D1336182

'Who Is Vera Ke[...] [...]tail, filled with suspense, and brings to life a young woman who d[...] f[...] the stereotype of the glamorous male hero that has been, more often than not, the public face of fictional espionage since the inception of the genre. It's a joy to lose yourself while discovering Vera'
– **Anmiryam Budner, Main Point Books**

Praise for *Vera Kelly Is Not A Mystery*

'Knecht's excellent sequel… This winning literary page-turner gives a strong sense of a smart, queer, and complex person navigating an unfriendly world'
– *Publishers Weekly*

'Knecht's prose is lively in moments of action… Readers will be thrilled by Vera Kelly's return. A worthy and welcome continuation of a subversive series'
– *Kirkus*

'Rosalie Knecht is an audacious talent, and her latest novel a propulsive, subversive gem. [Vera is] one of the most compelling and complex characters in modern fiction… an intriguing mystery that will keep you guessing until the very end'
– **Lauren Wilkinson, author of *American Spy***

'Rosalie Knecht has resurrected the detective novel for the 21st century. Sharp, self-possessed, and with a nuanced, meaningful knowledge of realities and histories well beyond her own, Kelly's take on who's lying and why makes for riveting reading in every scene. I tore through this book. More Vera Kelly, please'
– **Idra Novey, author of *Those Who Knew***

'Impossible to put down and just begging for a third instalment'
– *Bookpage*

Also by Rosalie Knecht

Vera Kelly Is Not a Mystery
Relief Map

who is Vera Kelly?

ROSALIE KNECHT

VERVE BOOKS

First published in 2021 by Verve Books,
an imprint of The Crime & Mystery Club Ltd,
Harpenden, UK

vervebooks.co.uk
@Verve_Books

A CIP catalogue record for this book is available from the British
Library.
This is a work of fiction. Names, characters, places, and incidents either are the
product of the author's imagination or are used fictitiously, and any
resemblance to actual persons, living or dead, businesses, companies,
events or locales is entirely coincidental.

ISBN
978-0-85730-810-8 (Paperback)
978-0-85730-811-5 (Ebook)

2 4 6 8 10 9 7 5 3 1

Printed and bound in Great Britain by Severn, Gloucester

For Mark Joseph Leonida
and in memory of his father,
Deacon Clod M. Leonida

OCTOBER 1957. CHEVY CHASE, MARYLAND

On a Tuesday I came home from school to an empty house, watched the evening news, and then took two Equanil caplets lifted from my mother. Nothing happened, so after an hour I took three more, and then maybe more after that, I can't remember. My mother came home from work after a late evening laying out a special issue of the magazine and found the decorative fish tank in the front hall smashed on its stand and the fish on the carpet. I had apparently stumbled and fallen against it in my stupor, and then climbed the stairs to my room and sat down to write a letter to my friend Joanne. My mother found me passed out on my desk, drooling on my stationery set. She told me all this when I woke up at 4:00 AM in the hospital. 'You know you can't talk to her, Vera,' she said. She had a journalist's eye for detail.

The doctor kept me in the hospital for two days, and when I came home I was down like I had never been before. They had pumped my stomach, and it felt like everything inside of me had been thoroughly blended with a milkshake machine and then poured out. I was discharged on an overcast Friday morning when my mother was at work, so the housekeeper, Mrs Cooper, picked me up in the car. She brought me chicken broth in a thermos. I was wearing the clothes I'd been admitted in, a blue sweater that I had to throw away when I got home because there was dry vomit all down the sleeve.

I lived in Chevy Chase, Maryland, in a brick house on a corner lot with a beech tree in front. My window was the one all the way to the left, hidden behind the leaves in the summer. There were flagstones going up to the front door. It was a very nice house, which I didn't realize at the time because it looked like all the other houses in the neighborhood, and I'd never lived anywhere else.

JANUARY 1966. BUENOS AIRES, ARGENTINA

I met with Nico Fermetti in his kitchen on a Thursday evening after dinner, the two of us sitting in chairs pulled up to a Formica table with a chrome band around the edge. The surface was bubbled and bleached in places from cigarette burns, the pocks in the plastic left over after the ash had been scrubbed out. Nico's wife hovered at the stove, which he didn't seem to mind. I didn't like it. I saw no reason to trust her, and she was clearly suspicious of me. I couldn't guess who Nico had told her I was.

I had brought my things in a small, gray hard case, which I kept beside my chair. Señora Fermetti silently offered me a cup of instant coffee with hot milk. I thanked her, although she'd already turned her back, and then burned my lips on the drink and set it down. Argentines never seemed to have this problem. I'd spent the two weeks I'd been in-country with the roof of my mouth perpetually scalded.

'Let's see the toys, Anne,' Nico said.

'She has to go,' I said, in English.

'Puf,' he said, waving his hand dismissively.

'It's a rule,' I said.

Nico was very tall, well over six feet with a long torso that sloped down to a heavy gut. He had a large bald head and a dark mustache, and bad posture that might put people at ease. He was the contact Gerry had told me about. Officially, he was a foreman for a massive construction firm called Aliadas S.A. Unofficially, he was the man that the president of Aliadas S.A. called if he had a problem. Nico knew everyone and could fix anything. He had spent his life in this working-class neighborhood in Buenos Aires, which meant that he knew every union from the ground up, and he had built houses for the rich for twenty years, which meant he knew the old-money families who summered in Punta del Este and Mar del Plata, the core of the Buenos Aires elite. The president of Aliadas was friendly with the CIA because Communists haunted his dreams. He lived in fear of the nationalization of his company, and some said that as rumors of a coup began to circulate he had started to import rifles from Brazil to his ranch in Corrientes. In defense of his interests, he offered the time and expertise of Nico Fermetti to the CIA.

Nico sighed and murmured a few words to his wife. She looked at me hatefully and went out to the living room. I heard the TV snap on, and then the sound of a mournful full-throated male warble. The singer was popular, but I couldn't remember his name.

'You're very casual,' I said to Nico, still in English. I could just see the edge of his wife's gray permanent through the doorway.

The angel Gabriel watched me balefully from a framed print above her wingback chair.

'This is my home,' he said.

I lifted the hard case onto the table and snapped it open. I let it sit there open for a moment. I was proud of the bugs. I packed them carefully and lingered over them, and I enjoyed the effect they had on the few people I could show them to. There were nearly three dozen of them, wrapped in cotton batting, beside my other equipment – my transceiver and soldering kit and the extra rolls of wire.

'No bigger than buttons,' Nico said.

I lifted out the six on top. Each membrane was the size of a quarter, with a half-wavelength antenna of four and a quarter inches.

'You could sew it into a jacket, it's so small,' he said. He looked yearningly at them. I set one in his open palm. 'It weighs nothing,' he said, waving his hand gently up and down. 'These days, my God, the technology.'

'They're simple,' I said. 'The basic design is twenty years old already.'

'My children must all study electronics,' he said.

The coffee had cooled enough to drink. I sipped it and watched him turn the object over in his thick hands. I had dreams sometimes that I was walking through a mansion decorated with crumbling plaster moldings of fruit and vines and flowers, and there were bugs glowing through the baseboards in rows, pulsing.

'I have thirty-five of them,' I said. 'They can be set two inches deep behind wood or plaster. You can go three or four inches behind plastic. They told me you have access to the buildings.'

'I have access to everything,' he said. Aliadas had the contracts for every federal and city building, and Nico could map the wiring of the light switches in the Congreso Nacional for you, or tell you how recently the bathrooms in the presidential palace had been painted, if you gave him a few hours to make phone calls. Nico's apartment was modest, perched in a three-story building on a side street in Barracas, but there were small touches that gave him away as a big man. The television was color. Lladró pieces lined the walnut-stained mantel in the living room, pastel sculptures of young women engaged in clean-looking farmwork: girl in kerchief with goose, girl in bonnet with goat. In the place of honor, at a startling twelve inches tall, was a clown weighed down with dinner-plate buttons and a ruff, playing a mandolin. I knew how much those cost, and they had to be shipped in from Spain wrapped in yards of quilted padding. The señora's purchases, of course, and most likely the reason she was willing to tolerate visits like mine at all.

'We've had some success with dummy phone jacks,' I said. 'You hide the bug behind the plate.'

'Marvelous!' He laughed delightedly.

'You're too loud,' called his wife from the other room in Spanish. 'The neighbors will complain.'

He ignored her. 'Where are you living?' he said.

'I have a flat in San Telmo.'

'They give you a nice salary?' he said, raising his eyebrows. San Telmo was an expensive neighborhood.

'A dollar goes pretty far,' I said, evading. Inflation was at 30 percent. He glanced up at me, and I realized that it was rude to mention the weakness of the peso. 'It's a small apartment,' I added quickly.

He set the bug down on the table, measured it with his hands, and then lit a cigarette. He gazed into the bug, as if the membrane were an eye. 'This is my new girlfriend,' he said.

'I'm glad you like it,' I said, glancing at the clock. It was getting late, and the buses ran less and less regularly as midnight approached. I returned the bug to its layer of batting.

Nico stared thoughtfully at the hard case. 'Well,' he said. 'Tomorrow

I'll make calls. I'll find out what work orders we have in. Then I'll talk to you. We'll meet at the Plaza del Congreso tomorrow evening, all right? It's too hot to be inside. Seven o'clock, at the corner of Montevideo and Rivadavia.'

'Okay,' I said.

'You can find your way back?' he said.

'Of course,' I said. I leaned toward the door to the living room and smiled brightly at the señora. 'Thank you so much for welcoming me into your home,' I said in Spanish. She gave me a contemptuous look. Nico walked me to the door, kissed me on the cheek, and sent me out into the underlit hallway.

'Seven,' he said.

I stood a long time waiting for the elevator, which did not come. Someone had probably left the gate unlatched on the ground floor, which meant the wood-paneled cubicle would sulk in the narrow lobby until someone came by to reset the latch. I made my way down the stairs in near-total darkness.

It was ten o'clock and had been dark for less than ninety minutes. The sky was still violet above the low white buildings across the street. It was late January, the height of the South American summer, and even in the dark the sidewalks radiated heat. I paused in front of the building to search my handbag for a cigarette, and this tiny effort instantly started me sweating again, the silk of my blouse clinging to my spine. Back home, my radiators had become temperamental, and I had been trying to warm my bedroom with a kerosene heater that I worried might gas me in my sleep. In Buenos Aires the temperature hadn't dropped below eighty degrees in a week, and the shock to my system was considerable. In the afternoons, when the heat was most intense, I took naps in the bathtub in my San Telmo apartment. The air of the city, laden with the pollen of jacaranda and palo borracho and diesel from idling buses, had given me a persistent cough that I was aggravating with imported American cigarettes.

Nico might be all right. His wife might be all right too, for that matter. She was, after all, very scrupulously showing me exactly what she thought of me. That kind of honesty put my mind at ease. I looked up at the windows of their apartment, lit and slatted with venetian blinds – yellow light from the kitchen, blue from the living room where the señora was still watching television. What had Gerry said? 'When Nico helps you, he really helps you.' A negative corollary hanging there, unsaid.

I had to prepare for my work at the Universidad Central, one of the largest public universities in Buenos Aires. Gerry had briefed me. The CIA had been getting reports for years that the KGB was recruiting among the Marxist students. Marx was au courant, a strange handmaiden to Freud in the echoing hallways of the UC. Most of the Communists among the students were harmless, but some were KGB, and in the last six months there had been signs that Moscow had issued orders to activate. I had been given extra money to pay the foreign student fees at the Facultad de Psicología. I was enrolled in two courses for the fall semester. I marveled that after all this time, and under these circumstances, I was going to college.

I walked along Alvarado, mapping and remapping my route back to the bus that had dropped me off. Most of the streetlights in Barracas were out. Most of the streetlights across the city were out quite a lot of the time. In Barracas there was little to relieve the darkness but the light from ground-floor windows, and many households had already gone to bed. At the corner of Vieytes a shop was still open, and the proprietor and I regarded each other with muted surprise – a woman walking alone so late, a shopkeeper with his gate still up after the dinner hour. It was one of the makeshift, all-purpose shops common outside the Centro, the front room of a house made over with a counter and a few racks of packaged sweets, a shelf of flour and oil and newspapers, crates of Quilmes beer stacked beside the door that led to the parlor behind. A scene of domestic harmony was just visible through the doorway: a dog lying on a hook rug in front of a television. I felt a twinge of loneliness. The shopkeeper and I nodded solemnly at each other as I passed.

Always know where you are. The bus came quickly, and I ascended into the light. If you were left alone here, on this corner you're passing with trees on one side and a long whitewashed warehouse stretching away into the dark on the other – could you find your way home again? Gerry encouraged me to think this way, to constantly worry at the fabric of my composure. To always have two plans. If the bus broke down at this corner, I would follow the Avenida 9 de Julio north a long way to the Autopista 25 de Mayo, and from there it was only six blocks to my apartment at the corner of Chacabuco and Carlos Calvo.

I knew where I was. I could find my way home again, forward or backward, in any direction.

OCTOBER 1957. CHEVY CHASE, MARYLAND

The visits with Miss Kay started the week after the Equanil and the hospital, and were a condition of my continued enrollment at Bethesda-Chevy Chase High School. Miss Kay was probably not that bad. In fact I could tell she wanted to like me, which was probably why my first instinct was to lie to her. She was young. She was the counselor. She worked in an office off the home ec room on the second floor, and I had to go up there during sixth period twice a week.

'Do you get along well with your mother, Vera?' she said the first day.

'Not really very well, no.' I was being arch. My mother said that was one of my bad habits, and that I wasn't as clever as I thought.

'Why is that?' Miss Kay said.

I was knocking my knees together under my skirt. The skirt was an inch too short, but everything else was in the wash and I'd been getting away with it all day. It made me self-conscious, though, when I sat down. My sweater was itchy as well. I wanted to get home and take everything off and lie in the tub.

'She's angry at me a lot,' I said.

'About what?'

'About sneaking out, or failing Latin, or my friends. She hates my friends.'

'Why?'

'She thinks they're a bad influence,' I said.

'Are they?'

I shrugged. 'Maybe they are.' Joanne was my best friend. After junior high, her mother pulled her out of the public schools and sent her to a Jesuit academy in Silver Spring. We spent the weekends together at her house, and we spoke on the phone every evening until her mother made her hang up and take her bath and go to bed. We had gotten drunk on stolen schnapps three weeks before and been caught. My mother had forbidden me from seeing her, and her mother wasn't letting her near the phone. Being separated from Joanne had knocked the color and light out of everything.

I cleared my throat. I'd seen a psychologist when I was twelve, for about two months after my father died, because I wouldn't eat. The psychologist had an exaggerated expression of concern on his face all the time. We would sit in leather chairs in the front room of his house in Georgetown and a Pekingese would come and scratch at the door halfway through every session, and we would both pretend not to hear it. Miss Kay didn't look concerned, just absent, like she had a jingle stuck in her head and was trying to remember the words.

'I wasn't trying to kill myself, if that's what they told you,' I said.

'What were you trying to do?'

'Sleep. I have insomnia.' I had never slept well, and it had been worse lately. I hadn't slept more than two hours in a row since I was banned from seeing Joanne, and I felt half-dead.

'Your mother would like an apology,' Miss Kay said. 'Maybe

it would help to write it out. Could you try working on that at home?' I agreed to work on it at home.

I'm sorry for scaring her because she thought I might die and also when she first got home she thought someone had broken into the house because the fish tank was smashed. I'm sorry for the consequences of my actions which are that she does not trust me home by myself and has to pay for extra hours from Mrs Cooper in the afternoons and she lies awake at night worrying according to her. I'm sorry because I could have ruined my health and I am no longer trustworthy.

JANUARY 1966. BUENOS AIRES, ARGENTINA

I had found the apartment in San Telmo with the help of a motherly rental agent in a pink suit who had tried to cheat me on her percentage not once but twice, and reacted with a broad and charming laugh both times I pointed it out, as if we were flirting on a date and I was removing her hand from my thigh. It was on the third floor of a small building, so I could make it up the stairs when the elevator was out of service, which happened frequently because of the power outages. The other two floors were occupied by an optometrist and an elderly lady whose husband, now deceased, had been a well-known playwright. The rental agent told me all this in a whisper as we climbed the narrow stairs. I had told her I was a graduate student taking a year abroad, letting her catch an implication of family money in it, and she responded by vouchsafing the optometrist as an uncorrupting influence for a young single girl. My flat had a balcony, an old claw-foot tub, and not much of a kitchen, but the bedroom and living room – sonorously called el living – were spacious, and I liked the tiled floors and the tall windows. It was old and needed paint, but it had a faint air of glamour. The windows faced south and were hinged and latched, so I could swing them open in the mornings. I could swan around in a housecoat and drink coffee in a pool of light on the damask sofa. I paid the deposit in cash, with a bit extra so we could forgo the cosigner, and made the agent give me a receipt.

After moving in, I ate a late dinner one night at a restaurant a few blocks away, a place with white tablecloths where the waiter brought me a dish of sardines and a glass of sherry while I waited for my roast chicken. On the way home, pleasantly full, I passed a bar that made me slow my pace. There was something about it that caught my attention, that slightly hushed air that I knew well, a bar with a hearty clientele who are trying to keep their voices down so the neighbors won't complain to the police. A woman having a cigarette with the doorman saw me looking and winked at me, a lovely, slow wink. Her hair was short, swept back with pomade. I felt a burst of relief – a homey kind of recognition – and sadness, because I knew I could never go in. It was too risky for me on assignment. Things were lax in Buenos Aires, but the laws were sometimes enforced, and there were raids on bars like that.

After a week in the apartment, I'd made some small marks on it. I'd taken down an oil painting in the bedroom of a lamb with an aggressively textured surface, each tuft of wool standing out a solid eighth of an inch, and had hidden it on top of the cabinets in the kitchen. I had left up a print of Waterhouse's Lady of Shalott, because I'd always loved it, even if it was silly. It hung over the sofa, the anguished girl in her boat about to martyr herself for love of Sir Lancelot, the tapestry she'd been weaving in her tower trailing in the water.

On the jamb beside the front door of the apartment, someone had written an exhortation in pencil. It was a single cursive word with the accent placed, in that odd Argentine way, on the third syllable: Apagála. Turn it off. Meaning the stove, I guessed.

I imagined the housewife who had lived in the apartment before me putting the warning right there where she would see it while she was putting her coat on and digging out her keys. The stove was ancient, a narrow two-burner thing crammed in between a dwarf refrigerator and a scarred countertop, and I checked it obsessively myself since noticing once that the back burner emitted a faint smell of gas if it wasn't turned an extra click.

I didn't have much to do until I met Nico at seven. I spent a while studying the street map of Buenos Aires that I'd picked up at the airport. I was trying to memorize the Centro, in blocks, and then work outward from there, although most of my assignment would take place within a mile or so of my apartment. I sat with it through a cup of coffee and then went down to the street to buy a newspaper. It was not yet ten, and the full force of the day's heat was delayed for the time being by the deep shadows along Calle Humberto Primo. San Telmo was an old neighborhood, and on my walks I sometimes came across unexpected blocks of houses in the ancient Mediterranean style, with their rooms arranged around two central courtyards: one in the front for show, one in the back for servants and chickens. I had been in one or two of the grandest, which had been left behind by families that could no longer afford to live in such high style and which were now open to the public. Avocado trees grew in tubs along the porticos. Taxidermied parrots perched in cages among clumps of jasmine.

The more ordinary blocks were lined with low apartment buildings like my own, with high arched doors peering down over balconies to the street, pale gray stonework stained with the tar runoff from the roofs. Many of the windows at street level were open to catch the brief coolness of the morning, and I walked past couples at breakfast in their front rooms, pouring their tea an arm's length from the street, glancing out at traffic. Washington had the same heat but not the same closeness. The avenues are broad in DC, the houses at a polite distance from each other. I've always liked to look in windows.

I stopped at a kiosk to buy a paper and a pack of gum from a man with a leonine beard. I pointed at the stack of newsprint and then began to dig in my pocketbook for coins. He leaned over the counter and said, 'Which?'

I looked at the papers for a moment, not sure how to choose between them, and then he leaned closer and said, with a smile that seemed to imply many unrelated things at the same time, 'Left-wing or right-wing?'

I was startled. For an instant I thought I had already been found out, that the entire neighborhood around my apartment had been seeded with counteragents. Then the newspaper man started to laugh, and I realized that the question wasn't personal, that this was his routine with every foreign girl. He scooped up a copy of El País and folded it in half for me. 'This is the left-wing one,' he said. 'You're young.' I mumbled 'Gracias' and walked away quickly.

I was left-wing in America; I believed in civil rights, and I had voted for Kennedy. But by Argentine standards, perhaps I was not left-wing. I stopped in the café on the corner of Chacabuco, a dark-wood place with BAR LAS FLORES written in gold script on the glass over the front door, and ordered a coffee. I took it to a table in a corner by the bar and opened the newspaper. The president of Argentina stared miserably across a conference table on the front page, slumping forward a bit, as if he were too tired to sit up straight. President Illia's chin and nose pointed toward each other, which made him look even older and more unhappy than he was. He was a

24

white-haired doctor, sometimes depicted in cartoons as a sad turtle. HAVANA MEETING YIELDS SECRET PLAN FOR LATIN AMERICA, read the headline, and below the fold the president's spokesmen explained that the Communist powers that had recently met in Cuba were hatching a plot to foment Marxist revolution across the continent by encouraging the failure of moderate governments like Illia's.

'The Soviets wish to see a wave of right-wing coups across Latin America,' said the spokesman, 'which will cause such misery among the people that revolutionary Communism will take hold.' Gerry had discussed this line of thinking with me. He thought it was ridiculous, an obvious misdirection from the KGB's own coup activities.

President Illia was a moderate conservative with a mild temperament, and he was weak. Please be reasonable, said the sad face and neat, back-combed white hair. Even his opponents didn't have much hate for him. A few nights before, I had idly listened while a group of men getting drunk on rum in a bar near Avenida 9 de Julio called his administration a disaster, a tumor on the body politic, an economic poison that had left the peso in free fall and the material wealth of Argentina in the hands of foreigners. But in the end the loudest one of them said, putting on his hat, that Illia was a nice old man and he felt sorry for him.

I paged past a department-store insert of sack dresses with collars ribboned in white. The hems fell just below the knee. Direct from Paris, read the calligraphy above the models' hats. On the following page, a wall of minute type: movie schedules. The capital was lousy with movie houses, and on the hottest days they were cooled by whirring fans that drowned out the dialogue. I had gone twice to see women's pictures at the matinee, and housewives dotted the rows, neatly turned out with pressed curls and lipstick, faintly emanating perfume into the saturated air.

Farmers were blocking the roads in the provinces. CORTA CAMINO, read the headlines in the national pages, and there was a photo of some men with scanty, windblown hair standing in front of a row of tractors. Policemen circled nearby. The article had a tone of treading ground that was already well-trod, the roadblocks being a news event that occurred and recurred, in which everyone played their appointed role: the farmers with arms crossed, saying they could hardly afford to feed the nation anymore with export prices so low; the local officials giving a press conference in the mud by the side of the road; the vacationers, cars packed with children, aggrievedly turning around to take the long route to the beach. The vacationers hinted broadly that Juan Perón was to blame for all this, somehow, though he'd been in exile in Spain for eleven years.

Illia would be pushed out soon. The grumbling from the Argentine generals was growing louder and louder, and a hack magazine called Confirmado in Buenos Aires had been openly calling for a military coup for the last six months. Behind this, there were shadows moving – the Soviets, waiting for their moment. Gerry had told me in one of our phone-booth calls, three days before, that he had a name for me.

'Román Orellanos,' he said.

He was a law student at the Universidad Central, the son of a wealthy family from Rosario. The CIA had intelligence that he had recently taken a bus to the *triple frontera* – the triple border, where Argentina met Brazil and Paraguay at Iguazu Falls, an immense series of cataracts surrounded by tropical parkland.

The triple border was a smuggling hub. A station chief in Brazil had picked up chatter that Mr Orellanos had met a man on the Paraguayan side who dealt in cheap explosives. They didn't know what he'd bought or how much of it or what he'd done with it. They only knew he'd taken an overnight bus back to Buenos Aires the next evening. He was known to be friends with Marxist students.

'Orellanos is a big man on campus down there,' Gerry said. 'He's popular. He knows everybody and he's planning something. Find out what.'

In finding Mr Orellanos, I was on my own. With surveillance, on the other hand, I had help. Nico would give me access to the buildings, the Congreso Nacional and maybe even the Casa Rosada, the Pink House, which was the presidential palace. His workmen would plant the bugs. And I would listen.

NOVEMBER 1957. CHEVY CHASE, MARYLAND

After the Equanil, everyone thought I was crazy. And as soon as my sanity was in question, everyone was suddenly very worried about what boys I knew and if I was ever alone with them and if I understood what would happen to me if I got pregnant. They managed to convey all this without ever saying the word pregnant. Miss Kay and my mother and the principal at school just started giving me the looks I'd seen them give other girls.

I was sorry about the fish. I told my friend Angelina that, and she laughed in my face. I guess she thought I was colder than I was. There seemed to be a lot of people around who thought that.

'How many were there?' she said.

'I don't know. Ten or fifteen. Hard to say. They kept having babies and eating them, and eating each other.'

'Not much of a loss, then,' she said.

'It's not their fault, they're just animals.'

We were walking home from school down the avenue under the tall sycamores, which were bare. Angelina was smoking in her Grace Kelly way, which annoyed me. She held the cigarette up with a limp sexy wrist so it plowed ahead of her like a mermaid on a ship.

'That must have been something,' she said. 'When your mother walked in and they were all flopping around on the rug.'

'Knock it off,' I said.

'You're tenderhearted,' she said. 'You know, if you really were trying to kill yourself, you could tell me.' She pivoted to look into my eyes.

'I wasn't,' I said.

'Maybe unconsciously you were,' she said. She'd been reading Freud, mostly to irritate her mother.

I missed Joanne so badly that I found myself writing her letters at school, and when evaluated with a cold and neutral eye they looked an awful lot like love letters. I couldn't explain this to myself or anyone else. I still wasn't sleeping well, and school that year was less and less comprehensible to me. I was failing everything. I'd started failing everything in a spirit of experiment, thinking I could stop once I'd found out what would happen, whether the heavens would open above Bethesda-Chevy Chase, the walls come down like pasteboard, a team of psychiatrists arrive in a van, etc. I hadn't realized that once you started failing it was very hard to stop. There was no time. Suddenly my Latin teacher was keeping me after class for a quick illustration, via percentages on the board, of how impossibly excellent I would have to be for the rest of the term to even pass. I had forgotten my declensions. The dumbest girls in the class were far ahead of me, skimming over the filthiest passages of Catullus. They were quoting Virgil in the washroom after class. I was an idiot.

Calculus had entered a phase of squiggly lines. In European history I was four hundred years behind in memorizing lines of accession. Bethesda-Chevy Chase was very proud of its college acceptance rate, even for girls – there were many Seven Sisters graduates among the faculty, all of them slim, soft-haired, relentless women – and while I was falling down the class lists I kept finding teachers and administrators trying to push me back up. So I was in limbo, not quite flunking and not quite passing, not in and not out.

JANUARY 1966. BUENOS AIRES, ARGENTINA

There was a space-age ice cream parlor just off the Plaza del Congreso with a low white counter that swirled sinuously past the vats of ice cream, a subtle pearlized sheen in the plastic. Abstract shapes in mint green and tangerine and beige decorated the walls. There was a line out the door. I arrived early for my meeting with Nico, ordered a scoop of chocolate and a scoop of dulce de leche, and took the dripping cone out to the broad plaza. It was two blocks long, dusty and hot, with the National Congress looming at one end like a battleship at anchor. In front of it, a stone monument hefted a crowd of bronze figures toward the yellowing sky. I could make out a woman at the top, in a war helmet, raising a torch or a knife. A flock of pigeons excitedly traversed a dry pool that spread out from the base. A couple of small children were flinging bread to the birds, balancing on the concrete margin, while their parents watched from benches.

I chose a spot in the shade of the squat, jolly-looking *palo borracho* trees and tried to finish my ice cream without getting it all over my blouse. I cleaned my fingers with a napkin and opened the newspaper from my bag, pretending to read.

I took stock of the people nearby. Two women on a bench

with a baby I dismissed immediately, along with a pair of teenagers creeping their hands under each other's shirts. A priest slept with a black hat over his face. A man in a pink shirt and a chocolate-brown tie loitered near the rosebushes along Avenida Rivadavia, sunglasses on, sweat stains spreading from beneath his arms. I watched him check his watch a few times, pick at his nails, bend to tighten the laces on his shoes. Ten minutes went by before I realized he was loitering there for the purpose of watching the teenagers on the bench, the girl with her skirt hiked up and her leg slung over the boy's lap, the boy rubbing her ankle under its white sock with a kind of fixed hysteria, the fingers of his other hand digging under her patent leather belt. I read the comics again.

Nico materialized from the knot of traffic on the far side of the square at 7:15 and made his way toward me slowly, smiling, fanning himself with his hat. He was flushed, his skin pink against the dark mustache, and he was squinting across the raised dust of the square as if there were no person on earth he could be more delighted to see than myself. When he stopped in front of my bench, he put the hat on for a moment only so he could doff it with a gentlemanly sweep of his hand.

'This weather is like standing in a puddle of piss,' he said.

I watched his eyes move over my head to the glare of Rivadavia behind me, where the man in the brown tie was still standing in his voyeuristic stupor by the rosebushes. 'He's harmless,' I said. 'Not police.'

Nico laughed and slumped down beside me on the bench, which creaked. His trousers made the zzp-zzp sound of nylon. 'Someone has painted Evita vive on the ass of that statue,' he said, pointing to a bronze casting of The Thinker, streaked white by pigeons.

I laughed. 'He seems concerned about it,' I said, looking at the statue's furrowed brow.

'He's worried about the state of the nation.' Nico spread his arms along the back of the bench and cleared his throat. 'I've made some progress. We've got a few ideas. The phone jacks, like you said. We can get into two offices that way: the scheduling secretary's on the second floor and the senator from Buenos Aires Province on the third, because they've got work orders in. But there's one more, the big fish – well, the second-biggest fish – and you can't get in his office with some bullshit about the phone lines because he has them all checked every two months. He's paranoid!' He grinned. 'You know who.'

I searched his face. He looked very pleased with himself. 'Not Perette?' The vice president, a post which also served as president of the Senate. A lawyer and a bulldog, with a touch of LBJ about him, I thought. Rampaging through the Senate and clearly enjoying himself.

'Yes. He's the treasure we will work tirelessly to bring you.' He winked. 'We may have to make him a gift. Some new furniture, a picture for his wall.'

'He checks his phone lines, but not his furniture?'

'Phone lines are suspicious by their nature. Furniture is not.'

'And he'll take a present from Aliadas, will he? He doesn't seem paranoid enough.'

'It won't be from the company,' he said.

A flower seller appeared, proffering a basket of single roses, apparently sensing a smoldering romance between Nico and me, despite the gap of twenty years between us. He waved her away.

'It will be an English landscape drawing,' he said. 'Beautiful, original. Signed. It would be damaged terribly if anyone were to take the backing off the frame.'

I laughed. 'That's a pretty simple trick.'

'Sometimes the simplest tricks are the best.'

I conceded that this was true and pulled my cigarettes from my purse. Nico flipped open a silver Zippo. I lit the cigarette and thought a bit more about the plausibility of an expensive landscape drawing hiding a bug in the office of Carlos Perette. 'So who will give it to him?'

'A wealthy lady,' he said. 'One of the patronesses of the Teatro Colón. She's a friend of mine. This week she will discover that she is overcome with passion for him, and will send him a gift, and he will hang it in his office, of course, because his wife would never have it in the house.'

'She sounds like a good friend.'

'Truly, she is an excellent woman.'

I stretched my legs out, trying to air my overheated limbs, and began to feel successful. The Congreso building at the end of the square looked vulnerable and pompous, easily duped. 'Well, I think that might work,' I said. 'I heard of a diplomat once who found a bug like mine between the pages of a book in his study, and the housekeeper told him it was a trap for poisoning silverfish, and he believed it.'

Nico guffawed. One of the children at the edge of the fountain leaped down into the basin and charged into the flock of pigeons, screeching, and the birds labored into the air.

'You see that windmill?' Nico said. Across the street from the Congreso Nacional, on the corner of Callao and Rivadavia, there was a building in the French style – grand, with curving art nouveau windows and a façade darkened by the passing of traffic. A tower rose from the corner that faced the plaza, and at the base where the tower diverged from the roof there was a windmill, just the blades, fixed there like a bow tie. 'That's the Confitería del Molino. It's a pastry shop like a palace. Senators and deputies go there to eat sweets, and it has an attic with a few offices in it that nobody uses. That's your base of operations.'

I searched out the top-floor windows that faced the Congreso, each one fitted with a tiny balcony. 'They don't use it?'

'No one goes up there. I'm paying a few pesos a month to rent one of the rooms at the top as an office. It's full of mouse shit, I'm sorry to say.'

'I'm more concerned about interference.' The bugs operated by radio signal. The plastic discs were inert until I activated them by aiming a microwave transmitter at them, from a distance of up to one-quarter of a mile. Then they transmitted a signal back to me and my transceiver, and I recorded the audio on a reel-to-reel. I had taken a few test runs in my apartment with the equipment, and found that there was an anarchic universe of shortwave activity in Buenos Aires, most of it centered around the port. I had to do some recalibrating to avoid it, the hiss and chatter of cabs and policemen and tankers unloading in Puerto Madero.

'There's the key,' Nico said, prying one brass key loose from the ring he kept in his pocket. 'But I'll have to show you how to get up there, what stairs to take – and the door jams as well, there's a trick.' He settled himself back on the bench. 'The key only ever gets you halfway there. The rest is always tricks.'

NOVEMBER 1957. CHEVY CHASE, MARYLAND

One Wednesday I got to Miss Kay's office for my counseling appointment before she did, and on her way in she banged her leg on the corner of the table by the door, the one covered with pamphlets on mental hygiene. She was red when she sat down. She had an overfull cup of coffee in her hands and her hot-roller curls were unraveling.

'Bad day?' I said. I meant it politely, but it was obvious when she looked up that she thought I was being nasty.

'Fine, thank you,' she said. Under the desk, she tugged at her pantyhose. 'You're failing English and Spanish. How is that possible?'

I blinked. 'Is it – ever not possible?'

'Your Spanish teacher says you're passing the tests but not turning in any of the papers. And you won the sophomore prize in English last year, I remember.'

I had written an essay about the soul and the Industrial Revolution. We had been reading Dickens. In junior high, back before everything fell apart, I had been a star student in languages, the one they sent to translation competitions in the city. I had a Spanish tutor from Valencia, and then a French exchange student came and lived with us. My mother enrolled me in special classes during summer vacations. She'd had an idea I'd be in the diplomatic corps, which had been opened to women. That all felt like a long time ago.

'So, if you're failing English, I have to assume it's on purpose,' Miss Kay concluded.

She was being much sharper than I expected. 'No,' I said.

'So why are you failing?'

Because everything was so boring all of a sudden. Why did anybody fail English?

'I'm having trouble concentrating,' I said.

I was tired. My father had sometimes let me stay home from school when I told him I was too tired to go. He liked to give in when I wanted things. My mother in the doorway, rolling her eyes. He had been dead five years.

'You like to read, though.'

'Sure,' I said.

'What do you like to read?'

I considered. 'I liked *The Power and the Glory*. I liked *The Cocktail Party*.'

'So you have more modern taste, maybe, than the curriculum here.'

I wondered if she was making fun of me.

'Well, yes, I guess.' I looked at a framed lacrosse team photo above Miss Kay's desk. 'I haven't been sleeping much, you know, and I have to read *Middlemarch* in two days for an exam.' Tears were actually welling up in my eyes at the thought. 'It's a brick, it's seven hundred pages long. I'm so far behind and just looking at it makes me feel desperate.'

'The book makes you feel desperate?' Miss Kay said.

I felt stupid. 'I don't know.'

'Maybe there's something else going on. Something else

driving this – this behavior.'

We stared at each other for a minute.

'Why don't you go home and think about it?' she said. 'Write it out.'

At home I sat and tried to write an explanation to Miss Kay for my behavior, but could think of nothing, so I wrote down every poem I'd had to memorize the previous year.

I hold with those who favor fire.

Frost was all right. I liked Emily, though, for being such a crank.

This is my letter to the world
That never wrote to me –

Well, I could cry about that all day. Who couldn't?

FEBRUARY 1966. BUENOS AIRES, ARGENTINA

It took a while to set up my equipment in the small room on the top floor of the grand pastry shop with the windmill, the Confitería del Molino. It was an old accounts office with a CUENTAS stencil still just visible on the pebbled glass of the door. It felt like the air in the room hadn't moved in decades. Once I had pushed all the broken furniture out into the hallway, I was left with a tin desk and a wooden chair and two windows that faced the Congreso Nacional across the street. I arranged with the manager of the confitería to use the service entrance, where they took deliveries of strawberries and raspberries fresh from the provinces and still drenched with dew in the mornings, so I could go up the back stairs whenever I wanted, even when the confitería wasn't open. The manager had been told the standard story, that I was handling Nico's accounts for pocket money while my fictional parents bankrolled a long educational sojourn in Buenos Aires. I had a feeling the manager might also have been given to understand that Nico and I were having an affair. This was often a good cover, because it could explain all kinds of petty lying and sometimes inspired elbow-nudging collusion from other men.

I did my best to make friends with the manager, Señor Torres.

One day I came down from a morning spent over my tapes and collapsed onto a stool at the bar, smiling at him. He was standing beside the enormous brass espresso machine, arms folded, and its water-tower appearance gave him the aspect of a rancher surveying his land.

'I'm sorry for the condition of the office,' he said in Spanish. 'It needs airing out. I would have sent someone, of course, but I had very little notice from Señor Fermetti.'

'Oh, it's lovely,' I said. 'Just what I needed. And how lucky, of course – to be in company like this!' I waved at the vast dining room that spread out before us, brass lights lost in the intricate plasterwork of the ceiling, marble columns providing a gentle punctuation to the room, like an Egyptian temple lined with pastry cases. It was one o'clock, and the tables were filled with men in summer suits, relieved to remove their hats under the great beating wings of the wicker fans. They were jowly, most of them well into middle age: functionaries and politicians. At a table nearby, one man bore down grimly on a chocolate profiterole while his companion cackled over a clutch of empty aperitif glasses. 'Such a high quality of people,' I said.

He warmed visibly. 'We are honored to have a very good clientele,' he said.

'I'm such an admirer of political men,' I said. I leaned forward, elbows on the bar. 'You must know everyone.'

He flushed at the collar. 'Oh, I have been here a long time. And it's an important part of my position.' He searched the room, and then smiled. 'There is the Uruguayan ambassador, for instance.'

'How marvelous!'

He searched again. 'And there is the minister of agriculture.'

'You don't say!'

'Of course, of course. He is here nearly every day. I make up the tray with the brioche and espresso myself.'

'I love to sit in a place like this,' I said, patting the bar, 'and just watch the people.'

'It's a great virtue to be interested in other people,' he said. 'Especially people at, you know–' He waved his hand. 'The top.'

'I've always thought so.'

At the end of February the fall semester began at the Universidad Central. Having paid the foreign student fee, I spent the mornings hanging around the main university building on Reconquista, sweating more than normal, trying to look friendly and aloof at the same time. I attended survey lectures in psychology, which enrolled hundreds of students and were taught in huge, sloping halls. Psychology was the most popular course of study at the UC, each entering class bigger than the last; the syllabus was going through the Freudian stages of development in order, so that now, at the beginning of the year, my notes were heavily fixated on the anus. After my classes I would spend a while in the student café, doodling in my notebook and reading a huge volume of Erikson. The coffee was quite good in that cafeteria. The air was always full of smoke and there were rude things about the girls carved into all the tables and windowsills.

In that first week, I found the student directory in the library, a cheaply printed volume that was chained to a desk the way pens are chained up in banks, and looked up the phone number and address for Román Orellanos. I walked past the address on a rainy Saturday afternoon in a kerchief and glasses. It was a boarding house, a crumbling place with a PENSIÓN ESTUDIANTIL sign, a faint smell of frying eggs drifting out to the street. A battalion of bicycles was chained up in front.

I went across the street and had a cup of coffee in a café, sizing the place up. The café was full of law students, reading in the corners and burning their fingers on glasses of espresso. I came up with a plan. The pensión was only a few blocks from the UC law school. I bought a second-hand copy of a nicely bound Don Quijote and wrote 'Orellanos' on the flyleaf in pencil. I waited until an hour after the last law lecture had let out at the facultad, and then I walked to the pensión with the heavy book. The front door was propped open; someone, apparently having forgotten their key, had wedged an umbrella in the doorframe. There was a lady custodian at a desk in the front hall.

'Hello, excuse me,' I said. 'Could I speak to Román Orellanos?'

'He'll have to come down,' she said. 'Women are not allowed upstairs.'

'Of course,' I said.

She picked up a telephone at the desk and murmured into it. A few minutes later there were footsteps on the stairs, and then Román Orellanos appeared, as if he'd just been woken from a nap.

He had a sharp face, nice eyes. His hair was just long enough to displease a priest. There were hundreds of young men like him at the UC.

'Is this book yours?' I said. 'I found it in the facultad. There was only one Orellanos in the directory.'

'Oh.' He was confused, turning the book over in his hands. He gave me an appraising glance, which I met with a bright smile. I showed him his last name on the flyleaf. 'Oh, that's not my writing,' he said, relaxing now that he had sorted the situation out. 'It's not mine. I'm sorry you came all the way over here.'

'It wasn't far,' I said. 'It just looked so expensive, I didn't want to leave it.'

'Are you Brazilian?' he said.

'Canadian.'

'Oh! Your Spanish is very good.'

'Thank you.'

The custodian at the desk was beginning to project some diffuse form of disapproval, so I excused myself and left.

I could be charming if I wanted to. There were basic tricks. The main thing was to be vacant but responsive, to put up no resistance whatsoever to another personality. So in the grand halls of the Universidad Central I had the same temperament and enthusiasms as whomever I was talking to, and everyone I met had the openness of a student, and before long I was drinking narrow glasses of weak beer in the bar across the street from the main facultad with a revolving series of undergraduate girls and boys. My manner shifted, but my story was always the same. I was taking a year abroad, a little adrift, and my parents were paying my school fees, hoping I would stay out of trouble long enough to get married. The leftist students were sometimes suspicious of me for being North American, in a coy, almost flirtatious way. Being Canadian instead of American made me a novelty, a fellow spectator of the United States. They liked to denounce capitalist imperialism over glasses of beer, and I would cheerfully denounce it also, and they would all be delighted. Privately I thought they should be worrying about Soviet imperialism instead. There were reports coming in of KGB cells in mountain hideouts in Bolivia, safe houses for Stalinists in the high-rises of São Paulo, Communist agents seeded into the governments of Chile and Uruguay. The American objective in covert ops was to preserve democracy, while the Soviet objective was to nationalize and repress. I marveled privately that the students couldn't see this. They seemed so intelligent otherwise.

Once I knew Román's face, he was everywhere, as Gerry had said. His voice carried in the halls of the UC, and he seemed to be always surrounded by a group of laughing boys and girls. It was easy to approach the fringes of this group, which congregated in a bar called La Taberna. I befriended his friends: Juan José, twenty years old, also a law student, whose ambition was to open a law clinic for indígenas in the high desert to the west. He wanted land reform, he wanted the properties of the Catholic Church broken up and distributed to the people, and one evening one of the other boys interrupted one of his speeches on this subject to say, 'And the big ranches as well, yes? Break those up?' and Juan José left abruptly to buy cigarettes and refused to speak for the rest of the night, which was how I learned that his grandfather owned a ranch in La Pampa that covered fifty thousand acres. His girlfriend was Elena, and she was smarter than he was, a source of constant embarrassment to them both. She was small, neat, disappearing in a wool skirt and sweater, studying psychology. She lived with her parents in Palermo, and talked anxiously and intently about Simone de Beauvoir whenever the boys left the table. She dutifully suggested that women's liberation came from a neurotic fixation on the phallus, as any psychology student would, but I don't think she believed it. And then there were Hernán and Rafa, muscular brothers who expressed most of their politics through soccer, moving smoothly back and forth between the two topics as if they were one. The character of other countries came out on the field, they said. The Brazilians presumed, the Uruguayans lacked heart, the more prosperous teams aped European styles, and the proletarian ones had the light footwork that you learn when you play on pitted dirt.

When they exhausted politics, they talked about music. They all loved the Beatles, despite declaring eternal enmity toward the English for stealing the Falkland Islands, two frigid inkblots in the South Atlantic. The islands were only four hundred miles from the southern tip of Argentina, but the British had annexed them in the nineteenth century, and they were populated now by a few thousand English-speaking sheep farmers and fishermen and a great deal of penguins. Two small, book-matched islands, their fringed coastlines driving into the gray sea. In Spanish they were called the Malvinas, and their theft by the English, the daily affront of English imperialism so close to Patagonian shores, was the single point that all Argentines, in all parties, at all times, could agree on. A Marxist in La Boca was just as likely as a navy captain in Bahía Blanca to have a banner on the living room wall with the slogan Las Malvinas son Argentinas embroidered over the flag. In bad times, Argentine politicians had traditionally raised this unifying specter before the public, and Illia was no different. Every time the boys of the facultad got drunk they would explain the injustice of it to me again, ardent and wounded, gripping my sleeve.

In the midst of this froth of political chatter and school gossip, Román was often aloof, sitting at one end of the table, undercutting another person's point with a joke, doing casual impressions of professors, rarely saying anything that would reveal his point of view. Perhaps it was this withholding that drew people in, kept this tight circle revolving around him night after night. Or perhaps it was Victoria.

Victoria was Román's girlfriend. I met her on a Friday evening in the middle of March when I came into La Taberna with a book, hoping someone might be there to talk to. I had been alone in the top room of the confitería all day, switching between Perette's office and the office of the deputy undersecretary of internal affairs, a new bug one of Nico's people had just installed. The deputy undersecretary of internal affairs had discussed a dispute over fishing rights on his family's ranch in Corrientes all morning, and then spent the afternoon considering the strengths and weaknesses of the River Plate football club. It had been a long, dull day, and the tedium of transcription was depressing me, as it sometimes did. I arrived at La Taberna at nine, after my politicians had gone home for the day, and sat at the end of a long table in the back, near the radiator. La Taberna was cheaply styled to look like an Alpine cabin, with unfinished wood everywhere, the tables and chairs edged with crumbling bits of bark that put runs in girls' stockings. Dark planks had been sunk in the plaster ceiling to give the impression of half-timbering, and there were plastic cuckoo clocks over the bar and the empty fireplace, where they competed for space with a needlepoint of a cluster of snowy firs. The students liked La Taberna because you could fit ten people at one of the long tables and no one would bother you if you spent the afternoon studying there instead of in your overheated apartment, even if all you ordered was an espresso. I asked for a beer and a dish of olives and opened my book.

Elena came in at nine thirty, unaccompanied, and sat at the bar. I whistled until she turned around and smiled. She carried her wet raincoat and beer from the bar and sat down at my table.

'I'm waiting for a friend,' she said. 'Maybe you know her. She goes with Román.' I looked up, interested. I had so far failed to find out anything about Román that suggested clandestine activity, or even clandestine sympathies. Perhaps his girlfriend would clarify things, or offer a new avenue of inquiry. Elena looked at my book. 'I can't remember my English lessons,' she said, lifting it and squinting at the cover. It was a cops-and-robbers Harlequin called Cold as Death, with a girl in garters holding a gun on the cover, looking deeply shocked.

'It's about what it looks like,' I said.

'It looks like pornography.'

I laughed. 'Not quite.'

Elena ran her fingers over the back cover, sounding out the words in English. 'She was cold – as cold as death.' The door opened with a gust of rain, and Elena dropped the book and turned around. 'There she is,' she said. 'There's Victoria.' She rose in her seat, impeded by the edge of the table, and waved with both hands. I took in her enthusiasm before turning to see the object of it. There was a ripple through the few patrons in the room as Victoria came in, bright and pink-faced from the warm night outside, pushing damp bangs back off her forehead, a small curvy figure.

I would find out later that Victoria was twenty-seven, two years older than I was. That came as a surprise. I guessed at the time, I think, that she was twenty-one. She was blonde and had a round face, winged eyeliner. She sat down on the bench with a sigh and a roll of her eyes, dropped her bag on the table, collapsed against Elena.

'I've had the most terrible day,' she said. She clutched Elena's sleeve, and then straightened and looked at me, as if she had just realized I was sitting there. I wasn't usually taken in by this trick – unfolding an entrance in stages – but she was good at it. She widened her eyes and leaned over the table, giving me the customary kiss on the right side of my face as if dazzled and confused by my presence. 'You are…?' she said.

'Anne,' I said.

'Oh, I've heard about you,' she said. 'You're from Toronto.'

'That's me,' I said.

'Do you miss the snow?'

'Not really.' It hadn't snowed in Buenos Aires in fifty years.

'I bet people ask you that over and over,' Victoria said, leaning in.

They did. I nodded.

'You know why?' she said.

I shook my head hesitantly, wondering if there was some trap here.

'In Buenos Aires people think snow is First World. Snow is for Paris, London, New York. In the movies, it's always snowing.'

I said nothing. Elena nodded seriously. The bar was filling up. At the tables pushed up to the front windows, a group of young men, none of them over twenty, were shouting their orders to the bar. Every one of them was wearing a shirt that was too small, cuffs stopping short of the knobs on their wrists. Students just come from the provinces. Still outgrowing their clothes. I felt an opaque sadness.

Victoria smelled like amaretto, I noticed, as she leaned across the table to take one of my olives. As if she had dabbed cooking extract behind her ears. She looked at the boys in the front window and then, confidingly, at me. 'Isn't it terrible, the condition of our young people?' she said. 'None of these country boys knows anybody in the city. They come in packs like that and live in flophouses. It's disgusting.'

Elena nodded, also looking at me. 'It's such a shame,' she said.

'Of course,' I said.

'Such a shame,' Elena said again. She glanced at Victoria to gauge the effect her empathy was having, but Victoria was watching the boys in the window make obscene gestures at each other. I had seen Elena hectored on other nights for her tailored coat and patent shoes, her parents' apartment on a pleasant side street in Palermo. Her father was a judge. Hernán and Rafa felt they were closer to the proletariat than she was, because their father was a country doctor who worked in a clinic on Thursdays and Fridays in a port town on the Río Paraná, where the Paraguayans who ran boats out of Asunción alighted for treatment of malaria and respiratory disease. I tried to read Victoria for money, but it was difficult. She had a good raincoat, but a button was missing and one cuff had worn down to loose threads. But that could easily be a bohemian affectation. Her hair was neatly done, freshly colored, no roots. The smell of amaretto was persistent, distracting.

'Do you like Argentina?' Victoria said.

The students often asked this question on meeting me, but they usually answered it themselves in the next beat. 'Of course, the weather is terrible,' they would say, gesturing to the street outside where it was either too hot or raining, and I would say that the weather in Toronto was worse, and we would go on to something else. Or they would say, 'We are very poor now,' meaning the exchange rates, the import market, the cost of food, the tomatoes being sold by the half-kilo in stores because people blanched at the price of the kilo. And I would say it was criminal what the IMF was doing and a shame how little President Illia did about it, and someone would change the subject. Victoria didn't do this. She made no move to answer her own question. She sat looking at me across the pitted surface of the table, and behind her on the wall a cuckoo burst through the wooden doors of its clock and began a palsied orbit of a cut-out pine.

'It's a beautiful city,' I said. As I said it, I realized that I meant it.

I was thinking of my balcony and how my street looked from it at five in the morning when I couldn't sleep, the air blue, the city appearing to have sunk peacefully underwater overnight, the trees undulating softly, the birds muted and confused. At that hour I sometimes saw men walking arm in arm in the shadows of the buildings, brief clutches in bus shelters. All things flow in the end to a city like that. I almost felt that Victoria could see these thoughts, the fuzzy poetics of a person who would always see this place from a distance.

'We're fascists, aren't we?' Victoria said.

'I'm sorry?' I was startled.

'Do you think so, Elena?' she said, turning toward the other girl, who blushed.

'I don't know why you say that,' Elena said.

'It's true,' Victoria said. 'The generals will take over soon, and my father can't wait. He says Illia has no balls. I bet your father can't wait, either.'

'My father is for the republic,' Elena said. 'He doesn't want a coup.'

'Everybody's father wants a coup,' Victoria said. 'Why are there never any coups in the United States? It's a very fascist country. I've often wondered.'

She had sharper edges than Román. 'There's always a first time,' I said lightly.

'That's very clever,' she said. 'I like that. What a clever thing to say.' The waiter brought her a glass of beer. 'What do you think will happen with Illia?' she said. She had turned her warmth on again, and it clashed with the subject. I found myself paddling backward, fighting the current she made.

'I don't know,' I said. 'I haven't been here long. Your politics are very complicated.' I looked at my own beer and saw it was empty, as was my dish of olives. Her attention was scorching and suddenly I wanted to get away, to boil some ravioli in my apartment and watch television. 'I should go,' I said. 'I'm up early tomorrow.'

'Oh, I hope we'll see you again soon,' Victoria said. 'I need English practice. We could meet just like this and speak English the whole time. Do you have a telephone? Give me your number.'

I gave it to her, writing it on the back of a napkin. The two girls stood to kiss me goodbye. I had some trouble disentangling the strap of my pocketbook from the bench, and then I was out the door and into the street, remembering that it was raining.

NOVEMBER 1957. CHEVY CHASE, MARYLAND

Our house was often empty. It had been that way even when my father was alive; both my parents worked long hours at the magazine, and my afternoons had always been quiet, myself and Mrs Cooper attending to separate business in distant rooms of the house. My loneliness now, in my junior year of high school, had an almost narcotic quality; I lost hours of time lying diagonally across my bed, listening to records. Sometimes I went to my father's old office and looked at the photos in his desk. My parents' wedding photos were there – punch and cake in the wallpapered front room of my maternal grandparents' home in Texas – and their college yearbook photos, the two of them dark-eyed and soft, their faces impossibly smooth. My father's family photos were there as well, crooked and blurred photos of a ranch, of jagged mountains white with snow, women in dark clothes gathered in doorways. There was a portrait of my father's mother in an oval frame; it must have been taken not long after she came to America from Armenia, disembarking from a steamer alone in 1909. My father always said how much I looked like her. I had her big, confident nose, the tan that persisted into the winter, the large dark eyes with corners that turned down. My hair even curled like hers. She died when I was seven.

My paternal grandfather killed himself in 1919 by eating a plate of arsenic, which ranchers kept around in those days for poisoning rats. They lived on a homestead somewhere on the plains of northern Montana. My father was four when it happened, and he never talked about it. I heard about it from his brother, my uncle Clement, who came to visit when I was thirteen and told me about it in a confidential tone while my mother was in the other room. Uncle Clement's arms were thickly scarred because when he was young, a half-trained horse had dragged him through fifty yards of barbed-wire fence. Because of stories like that, I always had an impression of Montana as a barren waste populated with monsters, even though I saw photos in magazines that contradicted this belief – blue mountains, prairies dotted with yellow flowers, happy cowboys.

My father also had a sister named Beverly and another brother, Zachary, who had gone away to college on an engineering scholarship and later, as a graduate student at Berkeley, worked on a small piece of the atomic bomb project. He didn't know at the time what he was working on, but he found out later, and the information seemed to fill him with something like megalomania, a confused state in which pride and guilt were indistinct from each other and both were dwarfed by an enormous sense of personal power. He divorced his wife and then had a spiritual epiphany at Yellowstone – it had something to do with a bear – and joined a Pentecostal church, then married a twenty-year-old from Manitoba. My mother thought it was ridiculous. 'A lot of people worked on that bomb,' she said. 'They didn't all leave their wives.'

What was there on my mother's side? Mostly silence. She rarely spoke about her own father, and when she did it was elliptical, more scoffing and snorting than words, with a single point emerging for my benefit: you have it easier than you know. He was dead too. A stroke at fifty-four. 'Don't let me catch you smoking,' she said.

My mother was an elegant woman, but she had grown up in the pine barrens of northern Louisiana and east Texas, her father moving the family from year to year to follow the oil fields, and she could be hard. She beat me for bad grades, for the incident with the schnapps, for being mouthy and sad and not as tough as she was. When I was seven she bloodied my lip and knocked out one of my loose baby teeth. She cried for an hour afterward, and I lied to my father about it, telling him I had fallen off my bicycle. That was what I could do for her.

MARCH 1966. BUENOS AIRES, ARGENTINA

Gerry and I had a talk on a pay phone. 'I hear you don't have much,' he said. The connection was bad, as if he were underwater.

'No,' I admitted. I had already mailed my first batch of transcripts from a postbox in the Centro, downtown. The senator spent a lot of his time railing against his enemies in an emotional shorthand that made it hard to tell whom he was talking about. He spent half his day dictating letters in his office, but he had done nothing for the last two weeks but reiterate things I already knew: that the army was squabbling with itself over how to mount a coup, that the faction called the Azules was ascendant, that a general named Juan Carlos Onganía was head of the Azules. Onganía was a conservative, as all the generals were, but he was a nationalist as well, and it was not clear how pro-American he might be in the final analysis. Confirmado magazine had published an opinion poll, based on what science I did not know, showing that the majority of Argentines were yearning and keening for the army men to take over. I had never heard such frank talk of coups. No one even bothered to look shocked. You hardly needed spies for this.

'What about our friend?' Gerry said, meaning Román.

'Nothing yet,' I said. 'I'm getting closer to him. I met his girlfriend.'

'You must be charming them.'

'I'm trying.'

'When it happens,' he said, meaning the coup, 'how fast can you get out?'

'A day.' A few hours to strip my apartment and the office in the confitería of anything of interest, a little more time to get myself to a ferry. Then three hours across the Río de la Plata and down the coast to Montevideo. This would be necessary because the first thing a new government does is sweep the old offices for bugs. I would have to evaporate when the time came. If I couldn't get out that way, if they closed the port, then Nico would drive me up to Paraguay.

'Did you get the package?' Gerry said. That meant did I get my pay, which he had wired to a post office for me.

'Yes, thank you.'

March was the beginning of fall. The afternoons were still killingly hot, but the mornings were cooler, and a breeze sometimes came in through my open French doors. The optometrist two floors down had pulled me aside in the foyer and given me a scolding about keeping them open all night.

'This is a real country,' he kept saying, 'not a playland.' He said it in English, and I wasn't sure what he meant by 'playland,' although of course I could grasp that he wanted me to keep my windows locked. I just couldn't stand to do it, since the night breeze was the only way to cool the apartment.

On one of the last really hot days, I knocked off early from my equipment in the top room at the confitería and wandered for a few blocks, lost in thoughts of my favorite haunts. I missed the Bracken, and Calliope's, and the basement of Bar 32. I was tempted to go to the place with the unmarked awning I had seen in San Telmo when I first arrived, to look for girls. But that was stupid, a fantasy, an intolerable risk. I stood for a few minutes at the corner of a park, having a cigarette under a date palm, thinking miserably about how long it had been since I had lain in the dark with someone I liked.

When the cigarette was done, I put out my self-pity like a light and walked two blocks to an ordinary bar where I could try to cool down. The tables in front were filled with expatriate Americans. After a while, a mod type from Houston started to flirt with me, a man with glasses and a double-breasted jacket in a ridiculous color that he had laid carefully over the back of a chair. His name was James. He bought me a fernet and did not, to my relief, try to explain to me what it was. Expat men had a mania for explaining the indigenous liquors.

'Did you know she built a miniature city out there?' he said after we'd had a couple of thick, black drinks. 'On the pampas.'

'Who?' I murmured. It had gotten dark while we were talking, and I actually felt relaxed. He was good-looking; I thought I could guess what kind of boy he'd been in high school.

'Eva Perón,' he said. 'A miniature city called the República de los Niños. With a tiny little post office and a tiny little Congress. They take busloads of kids out there to learn about democracy and weep over Evita.'

'Really?'

'I was there,' he said. 'They don't take care of it properly. There are rats.' He drank the last of his fernet and signaled to the waiter. 'This stuff is like medicine.'

'It certainly clears out the lungs,' I said.

'Two more?'

'Two more,' I said, and the waiter pushed slowly off from the bar like it was the side of a pool. 'My neighbor told me I have to be careful because this city is not a playland. You think that's what he meant?'

'This is not the República de los Niños, that's for sure.' He toasted me with his empty glass. 'Hardly a república at all, really.'

I moved to go at eleven o'clock, and he followed me out to the sidewalk, offering to call me a cab, hanging on to my arm, then bundling me into a kiss for a moment beneath the awning. 'I'll take you out,' he muttered. 'Tell me your name again.'

'Anne,' I said. I liked the way he smelled, and his touch was raising the hairs on my arms.

'I'll take you out,' he said again.

'Oh, I don't go out,' I said.

'How long are you in Buenos Aires?'

'Hard to say.'

'Come up to my room,' he said. 'It's just there.' He pointed down a narrow street. 'I have a bottle of gin and a bag of ice. Isn't it too hot to walk home?' He was tugging at my unraveling hair with one hand, untucking my blouse with the other. He was speaking close to my ear, so I could feel his breath on my neck. I had a weakness for that.

He lived up a narrow staircase, in an apartment that was bigger than I expected. When he turned on the lights, his expression was so hopeful and open that I took my shoes off right away. He had a good profile. I wheeled around his living room for a few minutes in bare feet with the gin and tonic he made me, joking about his furniture. It had been a long time since I had gone home with a man, and I felt like I was reverting to an old script, a script I'd learned from novels and films like every other girl: waiting for him to cross the room, watching him nervously refresh his drink. And then later, being small and breathless, and seeing that he liked it. With women I always felt a bit like we were the first two people to ever do what we were doing, that we were inventing it, that we decided in each transaction who we were.

I woke the next morning at eight, sweating in the overly bright bedroom, and put my clothes back on while he snored gently. It took twenty minutes to find a cab in the street outside.

I was hungry and thirsty, and my knees were shaking when I reached my own apartment at the top of the landing. The phone was ringing inside. I fumbled with my keys, trying to focus my mind through an incipient hangover, wondering if it was James calling. Had I left something at his apartment? Maybe he was angry with me for leaving. I lurched through the door finally and got the phone off the hook.

'Hello?' I said.

'Buen día,' said a low female voice.

Of course it wasn't James; I hadn't given him this number. I felt more clearheaded. '¿Quién es?' I said.

'Victoria,' said the voice, and then, in carefully accented English, 'I want to practice English. You teach me.'

She had said that before, that she wanted English lessons. I hadn't thought she meant it. It seemed like one of those things people said to be polite.

'I have an exam,' she said, each word slow and emphatic. 'All right,' I said. I glanced at the clock on the wall: it was a quarter to nine. I wanted to go back to bed.

'Gracias,' she said, and then slowly in English, 'I will like to talk to you. Thank you, thank you.'

Gerry dismissed Victoria. 'Fine, chat up his girlfriend,' he said.

'But we need more on him. We need to know where he's going, what his plan is, where his friends are. How are you going to get it?'

'I have an idea,' I said. I was thinking of the row of bicycles I had seen chained up outside Román's boarding house.

In order to carry out my idea, I had to modify one of the telemetric tracking devices I'd brought. It was the newest, top-of-the-line, best on the market. The army had been testing them on coyotes in the Nevada desert. It was small, a transmitter that weighed only three and a half ounces, a lovely little thing, but the shape was wrong. I had to take it out of the casing, rewire it so I could move the antenna, and jury-rig the casing back together at my kitchen table with a travel-sized soldering kit. It took me most of an afternoon. That was a Tuesday. I knew that Román had an early lecture on Wednesday mornings; I had heard him complaining about it with Juan José. He would be asleep by midnight. For all his sociability, he was a good student with disciplined habits.

I killed time until 4:00 AM, drinking coffee and reading a novel, then put the telemetric device in my pocketbook and went out in a dark dress and soft-soled shoes.

There were no streetlights in front of the boarding house. I approached from the corner, glancing up at the windows; they were all dark. If I was interrupted, I would bolt. I was a fast runner, and the gloom of the street was so thick that my chances of getting away were good. I gripped an adjustable wrench in my pocket.

A weak yellow light shone from the door of the boarding house. I walked past quickly, without glancing over. Román's bicycle, the familiar black frame with a red pinstripe that I had seen chained up in front of La Taberna, was at the end of the row, under an oak tree that had covered the sidewalk in fallen leaves. I moved cautiously, trying not to rustle too much. I was grateful for the dark, but it was hard to see the bike seat. I worked by touch for a few seconds, found the bolt that held it on and loosened it with the wrench. It took a few hard twists to pull the seat free. Beginning to sweat, breathing through my nose, I dropped the telemetric tracking device into the tube frame of the bike and fastened the seat in place over it.

It was done. I turned and walked away, hands in my pockets, pleased. The wrench had warmed in my hand. There was light in the sky, and the breeze that came before the dawn drifted down the street, cooling my hot face.

DECEMBER 1957. CHEVY CHASE, MARYLAND

My mother hit me when I brought home my end-of-term grades. She had me backed into the dining room, where all the most expensive and fragile *objets d'art* in the house were, and somehow it was the fear of breaking some of the good china and being blamed for it that sent me into a panic, more than the immediate pain or humiliation of the attack. I hit her back. She grabbed me by the neck and pressed hard on my throat, and I balled my hand into a fist this time and hit her in the jaw, and she let go.

There's a card in the tarot that shows a man in a black cloak standing beside a river, three cups of wine spilled at his feet, facing a castle that stands across the water. A palm reader in Union Station told me the castle is where he's going, but it always seemed clear to me that the man had fled the castle and was looking back for the last time.

That night I ran outside with her car keys and took the Packard. I made one stop, because I had some hopes; and then I drove straight out of Chevy Chase, heading north toward Baltimore, where my aunt Bev lived. She was my father's younger sister, and she seemed like my best chance. There was a tender spot on the inside of my lip where it had cut against my teeth when my mother hit me, and I ran my tongue lightly over it, back and forth, while I drove. My head ached from crying. The radio was playing hymns and nothing else would come in. They were up-tempo hymns at least. I sang along to some – we had been Methodists once.

Aunt Bev's house was on a corner by a cemetery on the fringes of Baltimore, a brick twin, the wood trim painted white on her side and blue on her neighbor's side. I parked at the curb and turned the engine off. A light upstairs was on. It was cold, and I wasn't well dressed. I stalled for a few minutes, sitting in the car. My conviction that I would be taken in as an outcast had begun to shrink over the miles from Chevy Chase. I tried to think what I might do if Aunt Bev didn't rally to my side, if she was unmoved by the swollen lip and the lack of socks, if I actually turned out, under her kitchen lights, to be a stupid child sulking over a punishment.

I went up the steps finally and pressed the bell. There was a patter of clipped claws in the hallway immediately, and then the barking of her fat, old corgi. Paws scrabbled on the door, and then a black nose poked through the mail slot. Heavier footsteps sounded in the background. 'It's me, Aunt Bev,' I called. 'It's just me, it's Vera.'

'Vera?'

An overhead light blinded me and the corgi rocketed past my shins, glanced off the porch railing, and circled back to press his wet nose against my bare ankles. Aunt Bev was tiny, somehow tinier than I remembered her even though it had been only two years since she last came to Chevy Chase for Christmas. She was draped in a huge red sweater with cuffs past her hands, and she patted at me like a large woolen bird. She squeezed my upper arms in lieu of a hug. Her wide gray eyes stared up through thick glasses. They were my father's eyes.

'What's the matter?' she said. 'Did something happen?'

'We had a fight,' I said. 'I'm not going back.'

She waved me in. The corgi shot up the hallway and made a sharp right turn into the kitchen. Aunt Bev, like a tugboat with a barge, pulled me after her and set me down in a vinyl chair at the table. She began searching through the cabinets, her back turned to me.

'How did you get here?' she said.

'I drove.'

'It's late, Vera.'

'I know. I'm sorry.' I was snuffling again.

'What happened?'

'She hit me,' I said. 'She always hits me, and this time I hit her back. I can't go home.'

She set a canister of Hershey's cocoa powder on the counter and looked at me.

'Have you ever seen her mad?' I said.

'No,' she said. 'You think she'd let me? Not our Liz.'

I wiped my nose with the back of my hand. I had no handkerchief, no Kleenex in my pocket.

'I have egg salad,' she said. 'Are you hungry?'

'Yes, please.'

She took a covered bowl from the refrigerator, a loaf of bread, a quart of milk. She made a sandwich and put the milk in a saucepan. She was making cocoa. For a few minutes she didn't say anything, and I began to think that she might not care what had happened in Chevy Chase. An opportunity to explain myself was slipping away. 'She hates me,' I said. 'She hardly talks to me.'

'I'm sure she doesn't hate you.'

'She does. She acts like she does.'

'She has to manage all by herself, Vera.'

That didn't make any sense to me. If ever there was a person in the world who had no trouble managing, it was my mother.

'She's far from her people, too,' Aunt Bev said. 'And I don't know how much help they ever were.'

The dog lay down on my feet. I was so tired. I put my head down on the table. My mother's people: a few quiet Southerners who seemed a little afraid of her, except for her sister, who glowed with scorn for her and everyone else in the world.

'What was she like when you first met her?' I said.

'Oh, she was something. She used to play tennis and then go and drink whiskey at the club. Lord knows where she learned.'

'To drink whiskey?'

She laughed. 'To play tennis!' She stirred the pot for a while, and then turned the burner off. 'Listen, Vera,' she said. 'Soon you'll finish school and then you can get married and you'll have your own house and you won't have to live with her anymore. But you know you have to go home for now.'

I couldn't look at her. A tear dropped on the table.

'What's the point in fighting,' she said, 'when you know you'll lose?'

MARCH 1966. BUENOS AIRES, ARGENTINA

Vice President Carlos Perette was not in his office the whole first day of the new legislative session. I sat in the attic of the confitería and read a newspaper, hoping he might come in. There was a long, high-flown editorial about the Falklands, and nothing else of interest in the newspaper or the office or the street below. I took a long nap at my desk. The second day it rained, and a commotion on the radio at 10:00 AM signaled the arrival of someone important – a bustle of secretarial alarm – and then I heard the low, barking voice of the vice president. He laughed a lot. His secretaries adored him.

'Four meetings this afternoon,' he said. 'It hurts my head.'

'Three meetings,' murmured a female voice.

Someone had canceled. Perette was losing influence, and he knew it; he could read it in these cancellations, senators suddenly away in Mar del Plata at their summer houses when he needed to speak to them. Phone calls unreturned. There was some shuffling, and the female voice was inaudible for a moment. I scratched in the margin of my notes. The reels of my machine hissed companionably. The rain had cooled the air outside, and I had managed to open both windows, after spending half an hour using a screwdriver to chip at the yellowed paint that sealed the sashes together. I had a thermos of coffee with me and a cigarette. Carlos Perette and I were going about our day together. He made a joke about how busy Onganía must be, the general everyone expected to lead a coup. That he must have more than three meetings today.

Perette sounded sad. I supposed he had been at this game a long time, and he saw the end of it coming now. I felt a little sorry for him, since he was one of those men who were made for politics – that was obvious even in the newspaper articles about him – and it's always sad to see a person cut off from the thing they love. I exhaled the last of my cigarette over the casement, trying to keep the small room as fresh as possible. It was funny to look across the street at the Congreso building, the upper floors at the same level where I sat, and know this conversation was going on somewhere inside. I always liked that.

I kept one notebook for transcriptions and another with special unlined pages that folded out to four times their size, which I used for making charts. I marked down new entities as I heard of them, and circled and connected them if they appeared to be connected, and it was always a good day if I could draw a new line between two old items. Pages and pages of this, and one-tenth, perhaps, would turn out to matter. One-twentieth. It took so much patience.

'You have reports to read,' said one of the female voices.

'Why doesn't he come to see me?' Perette said suddenly, his voice rising petulantly.

'Onganía?' said another male voice.

'He doesn't come to this office,' said Perette.

There was muttering that I couldn't make out.

'Pah.' Perette laughed. 'He thinks he's too pious to come here.'

'Oh, no. No.'

'You don't think so? You would be astounded how naïve the military men can be. In Bahía Blanca' – that was where the navy was based – 'they say he was in a duel in '43. Someone offended him, so they took a pair of dueling pistols out to the rugby field at the Academia San Bartolomé, with a priest and two surgeons watching. What a joke.'

'Was the other man killed?'

'I suppose so. Onganía is still walking, isn't he?'

'Maybe the other man was only wounded.'

'Perez, your concern for him is touching. It probably never happened.'

General Onganía's name was on everyone's lips. They called him the Cavalryman, or the Basque. He had resigned from his post in the army a few months back, and people said that when President Illia accepted his resignation, he 'signed his own death warrant.' I had heard this phrase repeated several times in the bars around the Avenida Rivadavia, tossed off casually, and it was not clear to me whether people were being literal when they said 'death.' These basic elements of misunderstanding, which were deeper than language, sometimes kept me up at night. It was so difficult to know what people meant from what they said. Was this a city waiting for the murder of its president? Or would he just be pushed out, sent to rest in an estancia somewhere in the west where he couldn't do any harm, or to Spain, where he would probably not be important enough, among the crowds of Latin American presidents in exile, to merit an invitation to Juan Perón's dinner parties? I wanted to know, but it would take a bug in Onganía's house to work it out, if Onganía even knew himself.

There was a noise on the landing. I went still as a rabbit, then pulled off the headphones and set them gently on the floor. The noise came again. It was a footstep, undeniably, on the worn stairs. Someone was standing on the other side of the warped door that stuck in the frame, the door that had once opened on a typing pool that formed a secretarial moat around this back office.

I put out one foot and hooked it around my tape recorder, which still hissed imperturbably, and pressed the stop button with my toe. It made a sound like a gunshot in the rainy half-light. Why had they not padded the button and the spools? I slid the transcription pad into a drawer, went to the door of the inner office, and looked out.

The knob on the door to the stairs was turning. I practiced an expression of irritation, my heart pounding. I had a right to be in this room.

'Yes?' I called out in Spanish. 'Who's there, please?'

There was a muffled kick to the door, and it swung open. A boy stood in the doorway, as still as I was. He was wearing the loose blue trousers that all the kitchen staff wore, and he had the obscene thinness of adolescence, a ladder of bones with clothing draped uncomfortably over it. He said nothing.

We looked at each other. There was a light on the stairs, and it shone straight down on the top of his head, so he was mostly hair and nose.

'What do you want?' I said.

'You're the Turk,' he said.

I was confused. I was gripping a pen for effect, and I pointed it at him. 'I'm the bookkeeper,' I said finally.

'The bookkeeper is the Turk,' he said. 'The woman Turk.'

I grasped that I was, in fact, the Turk. I remembered now that the realtor who showed me my apartment had called the Syrian grocer across the street a Turk, which I had thought was simply an error of nationality, but now I realized that it was a catch-all, and it covered me. You just had to have the right kind of face, and I did. My Armenian grandmother would have had a stroke if she'd heard it.

'I'm working,' I said. 'Are you allowed to come up here?'

He didn't answer.

'I'll tell the manager you were up here,' I said. 'Came up for a cigarette, did you? What will he think of that?'

He stepped back, paused under the light, and then was gone down the stairs. The racket of creaking boards lasted a while after he was out of sight. I let out a breath, shut the door, and went back to my chair. An ambulance was moaning in the street below, trying to push through the traffic at the corner of Callao and Rivadavia, and I was sweating from the surprise.

I had asked Gerry before I came: What happens if it goes bad? What if they arrest me? We'll make every effort, he said.

I folded the ledger up and lit another cigarette. I would need to get a dead bolt for the outer door. I could straighten that out with the manager downstairs; tell him there was private financial information up here.

My heart was still beating too fast. I walked three laps around the outer office, then turned the tape recorder back on and ate the sandwich I had brought in my purse for lunch. It's hard to be afraid while you're eating a sandwich.

I lasted only another hour in my post that day. It was evening when I came down the stairs of the confitería, carrying my equipment in a shoulder bag. I stopped in the main dining room, the salón, and the manager poured me a glass of sherry at the bar and looked around the room while I chatted; he wasn't much for chatting back, but I took the glass of sherry as a sign of friendship anyway. He made no objection when I said I was buying a lock for the office door.

The street outside had been washed clean by a day of rain, and there was a cool shock to the air. The season was really turning now, and I was glad of my nylons for the first time in months. The evening wind from the Río de la Plata was scattering the clouds, and in the new darkness there were patches of deep, clear blue in the sky. There was a sadness to this kind of weather. Was it just that it made me think of school? Bethesda-Chevy Chase, and then the year at the Barrington School, the year I turned eighteen, walking down the short path from the chapel to the dormitory at precisely this point in the evening, that deep, transparent blue in the west that was the blue of space. Wet oak leaves on the bricks. On fall evenings you were always alone.

Light spilled out of the bars on Rivadavia. It was twenty blocks or so back to my apartment, and I could have taken a bus, but I decided to walk instead, since the weather was so fresh. I had been thinking of getting a cat. But who would I give it to when I left? And sometimes I was out all night. I didn't like walking past all the men sitting in the open French doors of the bars, but as I passed I realized that the abrupt darkness of the evening had dazzled them, and they could hardly see the street at all. I stopped to light another cigarette in front of the unlatched casements of the Bar Entre Ríos and a man drinking a glass of brandy looked straight through me while he spoke to his companion: 'They are all thieves, of course,' he said.

The bookshops had opened their doors to the cool evening as well. A sooty cat rested in the doorway of one, settled in a crouch like a loaf of bread. A cart of used paperbacks had been pushed out on the sidewalk, and I stopped to look at the ten-cent romances.

The boy might have been a kitchen hand looking for a quiet place to have a cigarette, or he might have been sent up to take a look at me – by someone. By the manager?

It was possible. There are all kinds of spies in the world, certainly, and all kinds of subterfuge, and the manager might be what Gerry called a 'mother-in-law': a person who is watching you, but who works for no one and has no particular purpose in mind. But then, sometimes a person who looked like a mother-in-law turned out to be an actual counteragent. Better spies than me had mistaken one for the other. I pictured the manager, with his well-groomed mustache, making reports at a pay phone to the Buenos Aires police. It was plausible. The police might want him for an informant for the same reason I wanted him for a friend.

I bought two romances from the old man at the counter inside and went on. I would get a lock for the door from the hardware store near my apartment.

The streetlights were out between Libertad and Cerrito, so I walked in a brief darkness before approaching the frantic edge of Avenida 9 de Julio, the widest street in the world. White apartment blocks rose above a softening fringe of trees on the far side, and in the distance to my left I could see the Obelisk, a disorienting echo of the Washington Monument that had sentried my childhood, bathed in footlights on the plaza at Corrientes. The dozen lanes of the avenue were separated by concrete islands where people huddled with net bags of groceries, harassed on both sides by cabs. I always felt like a rabbit crossing it. I was on the second island, waiting for another endless light and watching someone a few islands ahead make a mad dash in front of a van, when I started to think that someone was following me.

It was the sense of a distance between us that was too fixed. A man in a gray raincoat had been half a block behind me when I waited, a few minutes before, at the corner of Uruguay; and when I paused on the curb at Talcahuano, trying to gauge the intentions of a honking garbage truck, there was the gray raincoat again, indistinct because the streetlights were out, waiting aimlessly halfway down the block. Now I felt sure that the same raincoat was behind me on another traffic island at the same distance, ten yards or so.

I'd had this feeling many times over nothing, so I indulged it without much conviction. I half turned toward the Obelisk, holding my hair out of my face as the breeze kicked up, and glanced back. There was a confusion of jacaranda branches against the lights of a hotel at the edge of the avenue, a pair of matrons with collars turned up waiting on the sidewalk, three glum boys with their hair falling down to their eyebrows. There was no gray raincoat.

I was being silly; I'd been rattled by the kitchen boy. The light changed, and I hurried across the path of a throbbing city bus. The wind felt gritty. It was unimpeded on the avenue and carried diesel fumes, brackish water, and perfume. With some relief I reached the far side, where the wind dropped down and semi-darkness returned.

My neighborhood had a chattering charm in the evening. The husbands and wives of San Telmo were on their way home, men walking from the subway station with a last cigarette burning, women carrying their shopping up. I stopped at a market on the corner and bought a couple of breaded chicken cutlets and a packet of green beans for dinner, waiting in a shuffling line. As I stepped out onto the sidewalk again, I saw the man in the gray raincoat standing under a tree.

He was a thin, hawk-like man in cheap oilcloth. Sharp-shouldered, not tall, wearing gray trousers, and his face, turned frankly toward the doorway as I came through it, was red from the wind and lit by the row of bulbs that hung over the bins of fruit in front of the market. He looked about forty. The tree interceded between us, its yellow leaves jittering hysterically in a gust of wind.

It was a hiccup, the moment when we looked at each other. Neither of us was supposed to do that, acknowledge each other that way, though I told myself – trying to calm the quiver of surprise as I turned left and continued up the street, pinned to the far side of the sidewalk by his gaze – that it didn't matter. It didn't matter if he knew I'd seen him. I turned in to the Bar las Flores and sat down to wait him out. It was an hour before I looked out and saw the sidewalk was clear, then made my way back to the apartment.

DECEMBER 1957. BALTIMORE, MARYLAND

In the morning there were two police cruisers parked at the curb outside my aunt Bev's house looking for me on a charge of auto theft. The following day my mother went to a hearing at which my presence was not required and filed a motion to have me declared incorrigible, which was granted instantaneously and would be reviewed in a month. Two days later I was serving a thirty-day sentence in a juvenile detention facility called the Maryland Youth Center.

When I arrived, I was ushered into a small room by a woman with thinning hair shellacked into a bun and told to take all my clothes off. She watched while I stripped, and once I was naked she uncrossed her arms and left the room and came back with a smock for me to wear, which had a number inked on it near the collar, and a pair of stockings much thinner than the ones I had come in with.

I learned later, from the other girls, that if I had had a pocketbook with me they would have confiscated it, and they would have made a point of destroying makeup. 'They don't just throw it away,' said a girl who had cut most of her own hair off with sewing scissors. 'They run it under hot water and mash it together in front of you. I had a coral Lancôme.' She shook her head. Her eyes were wet. 'A coral fucking Lancôme,' she said.

The Maryland Youth Center was a brick building stranded on a low rise, a treeless waste that looked like a scalp shaved for hygienic purposes. The windows had metal grates across them, which was to prevent both escapes and suicide attempts, although the building was only three stories high. I was told that the thick hedge of yews around it had been planted after a bad run in which three girls had jumped from the roof in the space of two weeks and broken their legs on the pavement. There is no place on this earth where suicide is more freely discussed than in a juvenile detention center for girls.

MARCH 1966. BUENOS AIRES, ARGENTINA

The day after I was followed, I went to see Nico. I rang his bell several times from the street, jabbing at the button. He appeared at the street door, out of breath.

'I must apologize,' he said.

'Too fucking right,' I said.

We stood for a minute, looking at each other. Anger was making me flush, and I was hot under the collar of my shirt.

'Sent somebody, did you?' I said. 'Christ. What are you worried about?'

'Mr Reyes sent him.' Mr Reyes was Nico's boss, the president of Aliadas S.A. 'He said he had to be sure about who you were,' Nico said, spreading his hands apologetically.

'We're professionals,' I said. 'Do you understand? Does he understand? You can't follow me around in the street, it could derail everything.'

'I told him it wasn't necessary. I told him it would be – rude. But he's a very powerful man. He does what he wants.'

'Well.' I glanced up the front of the building, and thought I saw his wife's face disappear behind a curtain on the third floor. 'Is he done now? Is he satisfied?'

'You're agitated,' he said, putting a heavy hand on my shoulder.

'I'm not agitated. I'm angry.'

'Anne. Please don't forget that we're friends. We're all working for the same side.'

'That's very clear to me. I'm not sure that it's clear to you.'

'Mr Reyes has been at this a long time. Wouldn't you expect he would want more than your word? More than the word of your friend, your Gerry?'

He lit a cigarette. A mail carrier went by, tipping his hat to Nico. We watched him go down the street. I would tell Gerry what had happened. It was not entirely a surprise.

'Come up to dinner,' Nico said. 'My wife made croquettes.'

I rolled my eyes. 'Your wife hates me.'

'Of course she does,' Nico said, chuckling. 'She knows a liar when she sees one.'

When I got home, I checked my apartment for bugs. I found nothing but some bits of blackened rawhide that a previous tenant's dog had cached behind the bathtub and under the stove. I told Gerry about the incident. 'Mr Reyes has always been a cautious man,' he said. 'We've run into this problem before.'

'Tell Nico not to waste my time with this nonsense,' I said.

I met Victoria in La Taberna for our first English lesson. I was early. Victoria was late, but arrived with a composition notebook and a ballpoint pen, which was disarming.

'I'm not a teacher,' I said as she sat down.

'Wot?' She had the British vowels that Argentines often had when they spoke English.

'Your notebook,' I said. 'I hope you don't expect a real lesson. I'm not a teacher.'

She glanced down at it. 'No, no. It is just – just in case.' She smiled delightedly at her deployment of this idiom. 'We talk, only. It is conversation practice. I write a word if I do not know it. Later I look the dictionary.'

'All right.' I flexed my hands and tried to look lighthearted. She made me uncomfortable; she was so alert. 'What do you want to talk about?'

She seemed flummoxed by the question for a moment. She blew her bangs out of her eyes, looked theatrically around the room, her gaze alighting on each person in turn, and arrived finally back at me. 'You,' she said. 'We talk about you.'

'Me?'

'Yes. You are–' She squinted over my head. 'Tímida. Yes?'

'Shy,' I supplied.

'Yes. You are shy. You don't talk much, when we are all together here, all the friends here together. You are shy.'

'What do you want to know?' I said.

She clasped her hands together and rested her chin on them, studying my face. 'You do not look North American.'

I laughed. 'I don't?' But I knew what she meant. I was the Turk, again.

'No!' She stroked her own blonde hair, smiling. 'I do, more than you! Like Doris Day.'

'That's not a question.'

'You have pretty hair. Curly hair. Do many girls look like you in Canada? Dark, with curly hair.'

'We look all kinds of ways,' I said.

'Do you have a dog?' she said.

'No.'

'A cat?'

'No,' I said. 'Growing up I had a cat. Not anymore.'

'What color?' said Victoria.

'The cat? He was orange.'

'Hm. I had a – how do you say. I had a nutria. You know nutria?'

It took a moment for the word to line up, like the pictures on a slot machine, with its meaning. 'You had an otter?'

'Mm-hmm. The animal, yes, that swim? With small ears?' Victoria said. 'We had a tank for her.'

I was swept away, thinking what the life of a girl who owned an otter would be like.

'Oh, but my friend, she had a monkey,' Victoria said. 'She would give to the monkey a candy of peppermint and the monkey would–' She mimed a shocked monkey, puffing air.

I marveled. 'Did you live in the country?'

'No, no.' She gave the name of a middle-class neighborhood, far out from the city center.

'You can have a monkey in Buenos Aires?'

'You buy in Brazil.'

The waiter edged close to our table. We had been growing louder, and he seemed annoyed by our exuberance. Victoria ordered a bottle of wine and he disappeared with a sharp turn of his heel.

'You are rich?' Victoria said.

I was surprised by her forthrightness. My answer to this was part of my cover story, so I was relieved of the trouble of making something up on the spot. 'My father is a doctor. But I work too.'

'I am a little bit rich,' Victoria said. 'My grandfather has a fábrica de gaseosas.'

'A soda factory.'

She appeared to have forgotten about her notebook. 'But you are rich in dollars,' she said. 'I am only rich in pesos.'

The waiter's black sleeves came between us, pouring both glasses. I tapped a cigarette out of my pack. The wine was dry and pleasant, and I realized I was enjoying the reversal – being the owner of the language for once. Victoria's eyes were very black. When her clumsy chatter ceased for a moment, there was her intelligence between us again, serrated and gleaming. I thought of a bar in Harlem, a place above a chophouse on 125th Street, where I used to go sometimes on payday if I was lonely. You had to tell the man at the street door that you were there to see Calliope and then you could go straight up the back stairs, which smelled like bleach and cherry jam, and edge through into a dark pine room where women circled in pairs. It always felt like it was four in the morning at Calliope's, and the dancing was always just swaying. Sometimes I picked up Westchester girls who had come into the city for the weekend, or I made sorties into groups of secretaries. Sometimes I pretended to read palms, and the girls pretended to be taken in. Parts of that echoed now: Victoria's sleepy affectations, her eyelids lowered and her chin resting on her fist, watching me as if we were old friends.

'What are you studying, Victoria?' I said.

She smiled. She looked over toward the bar, where the waiter was polishing glasses. I thought after a moment that she hadn't understood the question; she kept looking at the bar while the waiter folded the polishing cloth and tamped it down into his back pocket and began to page through his receipts. I was about to repeat myself when she looked back at me again.

'Politics,' she said.

I laughed and filled my glass again, and said, 'Well, that makes sense.'

'Your teeth,' Victoria enunciated, 'they are rr-red. From the wine.'

'So are yours,' I said. 'Why do you study politics?'

'Because I love Argentina,' she said. She hunched her shoulders happily, as if she had said 'the Beatles' instead of 'Argentina.' 'Do you love Canada?'

'Of course I do. We have so much snow.'

'You are funny,' she said, but she didn't laugh.

'All Argentines love Argentina,' I offered.

'No,' she said. 'They say they do, but they do not.'

'Not like you?'

'Not like me.'

I waited for her to go on, but she didn't.

'Some are very critical of the government,' I said. She was clearly used to being looked at, stared at. That made it easy to watch her carefully while she spoke. 'Juan José. Elena.'

'Of course they're critical,' she said, changing back to Spanish now. 'The government is very weak.'

'And conservative,' I said. 'Reactionary.'

'Strength is what matters,' she said. 'We haven't had a strong leader in – a long time.' I wondered if she wanted to say 'since Perón.'

'Does it matter more than policy?'

'Policies change, they come and go. I love Argentina, and I want it to be strong. That's all.'

Perhaps Gerry had been right. Her interest in politics was limited; maybe I was wasting my time. But there was a vividness to her that seemed important. I was starting to think that I couldn't understand Román without understanding Victoria.

DECEMBER 1957. MARYLAND YOUTH CENTER, BALTIMORE, MARYLAND

About a third of the girls at the Maryland Youth Center were there on grounds of immorality, which usually meant they were pregnant. Some of them were showing but most weren't, because once you were showing they would send you to St Catherine's Home in Delaware, which was a worse prison than the Maryland Youth Center. At St Catherine's Home there were no visitors of any kind, and if someone called for you they would say they'd never heard of you. I was told all that by a weeping girl who had given birth there four months earlier and been sent back to MYC afterward because she tried to scratch the eyes out of the on-staff obstetrician. It was because of the immorality that they took away the makeup. The pregnant girls would congregate in the dayroom after breakfast, and a woman from a church would come and teach them to crochet.

Then there were the girls who had committed actual crimes. I was one of those, I guess. There were quite a lot of thieves, but most were the shoplifting kind. My grand theft gave me some status over the girls arrested for stuffing Schiaparelli perfume and paste earrings into their coats in department stores, although I felt my offense was less intentional than theirs, since I had only been borrowing the car. Of course, if things had gone differently for me that night, I might have been borrowing it for quite a long time. But I tried not to think about that.

And then there were the girls who frightened the rest of us, whose offenses were unclear because they were so feral we couldn't ask them questions. One girl had cut a boy's face with a razor; another had broken her little sister's arms, both of them. Another girl, the one who most horrified and fascinated the staff and the rest of us, actually straddled the line: she was both violent and pregnant. Every third day she was taken out of the general population and confined to the solitary rooms on the second floor for bloodying noses or tearing out clumps of hair. She scratched at first, and then they sedated her and cut her nails. She would wait out her time in solitary, and when she came out she would be completely unchanged. She threw her relative freedom away each time with a new fight over nothing, which I thought was kind of aristocratic, how little she cared. She was showing, but no one talked about transferring her. She was like something painted on a vase, a pregnant Medusa. Her haircut looked involuntary, short like a child's and crooked across the bangs, as if she'd been coming out of sedation when it happened, and she was too tall for her smock, so it showed her knees and pulled on her arms, bending her into a parenthesis.

Sometimes black girls came in, but they were always transferred in a day or two to another place on the other side of Baltimore. 'They have their own place,' said a girl who had been leaning over me in the homemaking class that followed breakfast on a morning when two black girls, cousins, had been brought in overnight. 'They don't stay here. There's some standards, at least.' I told her she should shut her mouth and that segregation was against the Constitution, and she called me a Jew. We were knitting and not sewing that morning because a fourteen-year-old had made a dogged effort at killing herself with a needle the day before. The story was causing amusement on the third floor. They said she had been at it for forty-five minutes when they caught her, and had succeeded only at putting a bunch of red dots on her wrist, like a polio vaccine.

APRIL 1966. BUENOS AIRES, ARGENTINA

The VHF transmitter I had hidden in Román's bicycle was tracked through triangulation by two antennas, which I had to set up. For reasons of safety and convenience, I put one in the attic office of the confitería and one in the kitchen of my apartment in San Telmo. This second one could get the signal properly only if it was fixed to a hanging basket of onions that allowed it to angle toward a north-facing window; when the onions sprouted, the green shoots reached out in the same direction, toward the light. The device was very powerful. It was miles away, but it sent its pulse every ten seconds to my apartment and the office.

For the first few days after I placed it, I was preoccupied with thoughts of what would happen if Román found the device. If he was working for the KGB, he would, of course, instantly recognize it for what it was. My hope was that he would suspect Argentine intelligence services first. Student subversives in Argentina were regularly surveilled by their own government, and Gerry had taken the precaution of custom-ordering my brand-new VHF telemetrics with a casing that resembled an older, more widely disseminated design, which was used by governments all over the world. But my position was inherently precarious. I was foreign, my Canadian cover aside; suspicion could naturally fall on me.

As Gerry had said, if things went bad, I could be killed. And yet, in the place where my fear should have been, there was a blank space. I felt that I had been living for a long time in a place beyond fear, where my life was contingent and didn't amount to much anyway. Back home, I had known that if I was arrested at a dyke bar I would lose my job, and if I lost my job I would end up in a flophouse or worse. I went out anyway, because living was a dry waste if I didn't. When I started working for Gerry and made enough money to keep some in the bank, I knew that if Gerry found out I went with girls, I would be fired twice over – the CIA did not pay out to homosexuals, because they were too easy to compromise. For a long time already, I had been half a step from the edge of a cliff. That was how I lived. I did not look over.

The bicycle didn't move from the boarding house for the first three days, because it rained. There was a chill in the air on the morning of the fourth day, and I was dressing to go to the confitería when the signals came in that the bicycle was moving. I took my shoes back off and pulled a chair into the kitchen. The receiver was whirring on the floor, scratching out data on a roll of paper. This machine had been a bear to assemble – I had brought some of the parts with me, but had to get the rest from a wholesaler for office machines in the Centro and build it myself, as it wouldn't have looked right for me to come through Ezeiza Airport with the whole thing ready to go in my suitcase. The paper was sized to fit an adding machine, but it worked.

I worked out the coordinates from a reference book. In an hour he was back where he'd started, and in three hours, with my map and handbook, I had figured the farthest point of his journey, the place where he had stopped and spent twenty minutes before turning around and heading home. It took a ruler and protractor, and my head ached. He had gone to La Boca, to a strip near the water. The machine confirmed that the bike was motionless again, back at the boarding house. Over the course of several weeks the machine recorded Román's data and I worked it out at night, after my long afternoons in the confitería. He went to class, to La Taberna, to the law library. He went to Victoria's apartment, the location of which she had mentioned during our English lesson. And he went, three times in two weeks, to a desolate industrial block in La Boca.

The day after his third trip, I took a bus to La Boca. It was raining again, a temperate mist that could not be warded off with an umbrella. I tied a scarf over my hair and put on a pair of glasses. The bus was old, creaking and shuddering at its many stops. When it passed La Bombonera, the soccer stadium, I hummed a rude song I'd heard about the prowess of the Boca Juniors. The view from the window was rows of bright buildings, small markets, and then the blocks of warehouses that lined a narrow river, the Riachuelo. The bus lingered for a long time at an intersection while an old man in a horse-drawn cart slowly crossed. On the next block, I pulled the cord and stepped down. It was raining harder; the city fell away on the far side of the Riachuelo, and dark clouds were banked up over the low buildings of Avellaneda. A line of tidy houses stood to my right, which reassured me. As long as the neighborhood was somewhat residential, I was less conspicuous. I turned left and walked for a few minutes past auto garages and small factories, Y HERMANOS and E HIJOS written proudly over several doors. The foul smell of tanneries drifted over the street.

The block I was looking for was close to the water, and at the riverbank a few derelict fishing boats were casually tied up, like badly parked cars. There were two gray buildings on that block, both with small dark windows: one was marked WHOLESALE GARMENT COMPANY, and the other METALLURGY. The second sign was rusted; one of the windows in the front of the building was broken. Two stray dogs wandered companionably down the street. I walked to the end of the block and found the alley that gave access to the backs of the buildings.

No one passed. The longer no one passed, the more my heart hammered in my chest. I walked down the alley, a gravel track just wide enough for a small truck. Behind the garment shop, a card table and a couple of chairs suggested an outdoor staff lounge. The ashtray on the table was full. Quickly, feeling exposed, I carried one of the chairs over to the back of the metallurgy building and stood on it, peering inside.

'What do you need, miss?'

A woman in thick glasses and a worn dress was standing in the doorway of the garment factory, an unlit cigarette in her hand.

'Thinking of buying it,' I said cheerfully. 'Well, my husband is.'

'Oh, I see.' She relaxed, lit her cigarette, but continued to watch me.

'It's a mess,' I said, squinting through the window. What I could make out of the interior was a large, empty room, with a jumble of machinery on the right. Abandoned? I didn't think so. On the left I saw an umbrella, propped against the wall.

'The boys over there are quite rude,' the woman said.

'Oh?'

'They hardly say hello. One nearly ran into me coming out

89

of there, and he didn't say a word.'

'Where are they?'

'I haven't seen them today.'

I feigned irritation. 'They were going to show me the building.' I shook my head, climbing down off the chair. I returned it to its spot and rummaged in my pocket, as if looking for a key. The woman finished her cigarette and adjusted her bobby pins.

'Well, good luck,' she said, and went back in.

I worked quickly in the empty alley with a pick, and the lock gave. I pushed the heavy door open and propped it behind me with a piece of a brick. The machinery on the right, I now saw, consisted mostly of old table saws and grinders, covered with a thick layer of dust. On a table pushed against one wall, a bright spot in the dim room: a red can of Coke, brand new. There was a bright, sour smell of metal in the air. A track ran through the dust, as if something had been dragged across the floor. I followed it to a crate on the far side of the room and lifted the lid.

Inside was a bundle of wires and packages wrapped in plastic. The explosives from Paraguay. I stopped breathing entirely, then replaced the lid and got back to work.

The safest place for a bug was in the ceiling, which was criss-crossed with iron struts and the pipes of the ventilation system. I pulled on gloves and climbed up on the table with the bug I'd brought with me. Using a broom, I managed to place the bug on the top of a girder, just out of sight.

I hurried back to the bus. The rain had cleared, and the Riachuelo gleamed gray and blue. Halfway home, I alighted from the bus and called Gerry. 'The Paraguay purchase is in La Boca,' I said, and he called me clever.

JANUARY 1958. MARYLAND YOUTH CENTER, BALTIMORE, MARYLAND

Joanne didn't write or call, and I couldn't bear to write to her. I wrote to Angelina instead, telling her about the powdered eggs the Maryland Youth Center served us and the nasal drip of the girl sitting across from me in typing class and the weather during the twenty minutes of rec time that we spent on a fenced-in patch of grass that abutted the building like a chicken run. I had nothing to do when classes were over for the day but fight with the other girls or work on the letter, so by the time I sent it, it was ten pages long. In the second week, Angelina sent me a letter in return, a page and a half on the stationery she'd gotten for her sixteenth birthday, wishing me well in juvenile detention and describing the preparations for the Spring Fling that were under way in the student committee she chaired. It made me feel lonelier than getting nothing, so I didn't write her again.

JUNE 1966. BUENOS AIRES, ARGENTINA

On a cold afternoon I had been listening to Vice President Perette's secretaries murmur for hours when the man himself burst in. I sat up, coughed twice – I had been fighting a cold for two weeks – and scrabbled for my transcription notebook.

'Out, out,' he said. 'Get out, all of you.'

There was a moment of silence and then a flutter of footsteps and high-pitched voices. The door shut. I had never heard this unhinged tone before. I fussed over the wires in my kit, checking and rechecking the connections. For a few minutes the reels hissed in silence. I imagined Perette sitting at the desk, staring at the wall. Then he began speaking again. He must have been on the telephone.

'It's no good,' he said. 'The Basque doesn't want it, the son of a bitch.'

He meant Onganía. I lit a cigarette, fumbling with the matches. I had a feeling that this was big. There was a note of despair in his voice.

'Two million,' he said. 'A cabinet post, contracts worth another ten, and he says he doesn't want it.' There was a muffled thunk. 'Let him come here, if that's what he wants. Let him come here and get a bullet in the neck. We offered him two million and a cabinet post, and who the fuck is he?'

My headphones were cutting into the top of my ear, but I hardly noticed. They had offered Onganía a deal, and he had turned it down. He was set on a coup. It would have to be soon, now. Illia's government was out of ideas if they had resorted to an offer like this, and if Onganía hesitated now, at the moment when his strength was most obvious, he would lose ground. I sat up stiffly. I'd been hunched in the corner behind the desk all morning, and my knees crackled when I straightened them. I needed to call Gerry.

My favorite phone box faced a candy store on a side street leading into the plaza. I walked to it automatically, and then hesitated and walked past it to one I'd never used, on the corner of a busy, ugly street that amplified the traffic noise with a cliff of featureless modern buildings. A cold wind snaked along the pavement. The Argentine winter had a penetrating quality that wore you out, a fatigue from never quite being warm, the gas heaters on the walls struggling without conviction. I fed my coins into the slot and dialed the service. The usual woman answered and I asked for Gerry and gave the number of the phone box, and then hung up.

When the phone rang I jumped, and a man passing gave me a funny look.

'What is it?' Gerry said.

'It'll be soon.'

There was a brief silence. 'What happened?'

'A deal failed.'

'I see. Good girl.'

'I have some papers for you. Am I mailing to the same place?' I said. He alternated among various PO boxes.

'Let me see.' He receded from the phone, and then came back

on the line. 'Use number three,' he said.

I would take the bus out the next day and mail the transcripts from a post office on the outskirts of town. We never used the same place twice.

'Three, all right,' I said, and hung up.

I dialed Nico's number. His wife answered.

'He's not here,' she said.

'Will he be home later?'

There was a pointed silence that I took for a shrug.

'At suppertime?' I suggested.

There was another silence, as if she failed to see the significance of this guessing game.

'I'll come at eight,' I said finally.

'You will do what you will do,' she said.

That night I told Nico about the deal Onganía wouldn't take, and Nico got up from the kitchen table and took a bottle of red wine out of a cabinet. His wife was in the other room, administering some home remedy to a large marmalade tomcat with an abscess on its back, and the animal was making a continuous low growl that carried clearly into the kitchen. Nico found two glasses. 'Do you drink?'

'Yes,' I said.

He sat down again and pushed the taller glass across the table to me.

'This is not good news,' he said.

'That's what I thought.'

'Perette must think it's coming soon. He wouldn't make an offer any earlier than he had to.'

I sipped the wine.

'This piece-of-shit country,' Nico said, and I was surprised to see that his eyes were wet. He looked precarious, like a house succumbing to a mudslide. 'I tell you what. My boss, he doesn't care. As long as the next man isn't a Communist, he'll be happy. But me? Every time this happens, I age ten years.'

I fumbled in my bag for a cigarette. A minute of silence passed.

'I'm sorry this is happening,' I said.

'Oh my God, you should have seen us in '55, '56, '62,' he said, sighing. 'Every year, another old man shouting from a grandstand with all his medals on. "I've come to replace your previous old man." Some people would go to jail, everyone else would get used to it, and then it would start all over.' He rubbed his face. I shifted in my seat, then made a production of getting up to fetch an ashtray from the sink. I paused to look through the living room doorway and saw the cat, half its fur scissored down to felt, struggle free of Señora Fermetti and wedge itself under the dainty sofa on the far side of the room.

'I have to speak to some people,' Nico said. 'It won't be long now.'

'You think so?'

'I think no more than a month. Then Onganía does what he's been wanting to do.'

'I've heard he's very – proper,' I said.

'Oh, he is. The proper ones are the worst.' He rallied. 'Do you have another cigarette?'

I passed him the pack.

'She doesn't like it when I smoke,' he said, nodding toward the living room. 'I don't care.'

'A lot of things could happen,' I said. 'Onganía might fail. Brazil might take an interest.'

'He will succeed, and there'll be another thousand nobodies

sitting in prison,' Nico said. 'Students. Union men. Psychologists. The fucking children who write the editorials in the papers. He'll round them up and put them all in jail, break a few legs, some won't come back. You watch. What a fucking joke.'

'I'm sorry,' I said again.

'Are you?' Nico said.

We looked at each other for a moment.

'Of course I am,' I said. 'I don't believe in coups.'

'The Americans love Onganía. They think he's John Wayne.'

'The Americans aren't intervening here,' I said.

A small detail came back to me from the previous day: Perette said the American ambassador had chosen this month to go on vacation. I felt a pang of guilt.

'No one wants a coup,' I said. 'But it's a war, isn't it?'

'With who?' he said.

'With the Soviet Union.'

I couldn't read his expression. For an instant it seemed like anger, but then it dissolved into something multivalent, wry. I pressed on. 'Do you think they care about elections?' I said. 'Ask the Hungarians.'

An ambulance went by in the street. Nico rubbed his eyes. 'I'm tired. Do you know how old I am? I'm forty-nine. You would not believe how tired you can be at forty-nine. I spent fifteen years carrying buckets of bricks before I was a foreman, and now I wake up in the middle of the night so tired I can't get up to take a piss.' He sighed. 'What are you going to do when it happens?'

'Go. It won't be safe to stay. They might find the bugs.'

We sat and smoked. Señora Fermetti had turned on the television. It was Cleopatra. I could hear Richard Burton's insinuating voice.

'Best of luck to you,' Nico said. 'However it goes.'

JANUARY 1958. MARYLAND YOUTH CENTER, BALTIMORE, MARYLAND

By the end of the second week I started composing letters to Joanne in my mind, even though I knew I would never write to her. You are my best friend and I miss you so much. I can't think of anyone else I would even want to see when I get out of here. Everyone else could be blown up with a bomb for all I care.

Being declared incorrigible meant that I couldn't go home, and I had no idea what other arrangements were being made for me, since I was a minor with most of a year left before my eighteenth birthday and I still had to finish my education.

When I thought of Joanne I could never do better than a kind of wounded evasion of my romantic feelings for her. I pretended I was like one of the great ladies of the nineteenth century who sent each other genteel letters when they were apart about how desperately they missed each other. When we read those letters in history classes or came across that kind of talk in books, our teachers would explain that what read like passion was just the natural affinity of women for each other and there was nothing out of the way about it at all. Joanne had been my favorite person in the world, and when she hugged me and her face pressed against my neck I felt a fizzing, nauseous thrill from the pit of my stomach to the bones in my feet. That was all I knew about it and all I could have told anyone, if anyone had asked.

JUNE 1966. BUENOS AIRES, ARGENTINA

This was the week for settling accounts. Perette, in his office, was having meetings with every person who'd ever benefited from his friendship. They came in columns through the afternoon, were offered coffee, were offered sherry, had long conversations in which they either feigned sudden, total ignorance of politics or weakly defamed the president's enemies. Most of them claimed to have no power over the situation. I had never heard so many political men claim to have so little power.

I went out for lunch when Perette did, locking the door behind me and hurrying back afterward. I went only as far as the main room of the confitería. I tried to chat with the manager, but he had become surly since May, resisting my attempts to draw him out on the subject of the famous men who dotted his dining room. I was confused at first and thought I might have offended him somehow, but it came to me after a few days that there was nothing more distasteful and unwelcome to a person in his position than a sudden shake-up in power. He was mourning the four years of knowledge – of who was who and in charge of what – that was about to be rendered meaningless.

'What do you know about Onganía?' I said to him one day.

'Nothing,' he said, with a look of deep pain.

Some of the right-wing magazines were running profiles of Onganía, although none of them came right out and stated the reason for his sudden relevance. A few other military men were doted on as well: bets being hedged. The left-wing magazines were publishing editorials about the inviolable will of the people. They looked like they had been printed with more haste than usual, blank pages sometimes intruding in long essays, photos printed upside down. The editors were fleeing Buenos Aires already, leaving a few typesetters and stringers to manage in their absence.

June was the depth of the Argentine winter, and the city lay muffled and depressed under a layer of cold, damp air that never lifted, not even in the evenings when the wind began to blow from the glassy expanse of the Río de la Plata. I wasn't used to such early darkness with no Christmas lights to brighten it. Crows landed in the bare jacaranda trees along my street and stayed there all day, circulating languorously from one end of the block to the other in a giant wheel. The stray dogs that usually congregated in the evenings in the alley behind the confitería began to grow in numbers, sleeping nose-to-tail along the wall where the half-ton pastry oven radiated heat through the bricks. It rained every day, and the cafés were deserted. The bars frequented by the transit union were empty; the students in the facultad were reticent about politics.

'There were tanks in the streets in '62,' said Elena. 'People are going home early at night. No one knows when it will happen.'

My downstairs neighbor, the widow of the playwright, scolded me on the stairs for coming in late. 'There are soldiers doing drills on the parade grounds at Campo de Mayo,' she said. 'They'll be coming downtown soon. Girls shouldn't be out.'

While the city grew quiet, Victoria grew so loud, so manic and cheerful, that I wondered sometimes if she might be taking amphetamines. By the third week of June, she and Román were the only ones coming to La Taberna in the evenings, and instead of talking about Illia or Onganía they talked about the Falkland Islands and the insufferable imperialism of the British. I nodded seriously through these conversations, a little mystified. They seemed to be performing for each other, not for me.

The wall in front of the British embassy in Recoleta was defaced regularly, and in recent weeks, as he felt his grasp on power weakening, Illia had begun to imprecate the British thieves in radio addresses. In response, the British embassy staff had doubled the foot patrol in front of the gate. On weekends I saw teenagers standing on the sidewalk across the street from the grand building, shouting patriotic insults and basking in the approval of passing adults. Various generals, not to be outdone, gave interviews to right-wing magazines making veiled threats, stopping just short of promising to invade the islands should the reins of government be passed to them. A bartender in Palermo recoiled in alarm at my accent that week and asked if I was English, and when I assured him that I was Canadian he poured my wine for free.

The streets were deserted now by 8:00 PM, when the last of the office workers in the Centro had gone home. There was a sudden profusion of police, some of them looking too young to wear the uniform, still pimply, narrow shoulders squared in their jackets. They had been brought in from somewhere – reinforcements. On Fridays, drunk cadets straggled down my street, throwing bottles. Everyone I met had a story of seeing the soldiers marching in the Campo de Mayo, the base at the edge of the city. Endless drills, as if a coup were a parade.

Román sat in La Taberna and talked about the Falklands and the restoration of honor and sovereignty and the essential nature of Argentines, earth and blood, silver, beef. He and Victoria giggled like children, his dark head and her yellow one, his long arm draped across her shoulders. Victoria leaned in close one evening just as I was putting on my coat to go and said, 'Have you seen the boats in the river?'

'Boats?'

'There are gunboats at anchor in the river. No lights.'

'Argentine?'

'Of course, Argentine. Onganía put them there.'

This was the first time she had spoken Onganía's name in weeks. She seemed indifferent, most of the time, to the matter of who occupied the presidential palace and how they got there. Her vision of Argentina was historical, eschatological. She was concerned with its destiny, not the grubby shifts in power that were happening right now. She cared about the integrity of its territory. Its honor among nations, that kind of thing. A very long view.

'He put them there because he's a fascist,' she said lightly, rolling her glass of beer between her palms.

She sometimes cast glances at me when Román was expounding some point, flirtatious looks, as if she were inviting me to join them in their outrage. I thought about her on the way home, wondered if she meant these little passes, or if she just liked to see me blush. She sometimes wore me out, the way she needed to be looked at all the time. She chased after Elena's attention too, when I really thought about it.

Silly to think of her instead of the darkened gunboats on the river. I wondered if there would be street fighting. I hoped the boats and the soldiers and the hordes of teenage cops were just for show. Still, I lifted my mattress that evening to be sure the cash I kept on hand for plane tickets and ferry passes was still in the envelope where I had left it. I was straightening the sheets, reassured, when the doorbell rang.

I stepped onto the balcony and looked down. It was Nico at the street door. I recognized him by the top of his head, a ring of dyed black hair around a thinning patch. I went back in and buzzed him up, and then stood in the middle of the living room, thinking. Nico had never been to my flat. Why would he come here now? I heard the creak of his shoes in the hall and opened the door.

'What a surprise,' I said. 'Would you like a glass of wine?'

'Whatever you have,' he said.

His face was red from the cold, and he scanned my living room while he took off his coat, an omnivorous glance. The smell of alcohol rolled off him. He hung up the coat himself, not waiting for me to do it. I found a second wine glass in the cabinet under the sink, glazed with dust, next to all the other items I'd found in the kitchen that I'd never use: a set of oyster forks, a fondue pot, a Bundt pan.

'All I have is white,' I said.

He was paging through the copy of El País I'd left open on the table. 'You have something to eat?' he said.

'Well,' I said, raising an eyebrow. 'I guess I do.' There was a bag of biscuits from the bakery on Carlos Calvo.

'Let me have something,' he said. 'I'm drunk.'

'I can see that.'

He sat at the table. He moved like a dancing bear, a brain struggling for precision in a large, imprecise body. He kept a very straight posture in the chair, eyeballing my sofa and French windows as if they might be on the verge of saying something disrespectful.

'How drunk?' I said, setting the biscuits down on a plate in front of him.

'It never fogs my mind,' he said. 'Never. What do you hear, my girl? What do the birds tell you?'

I shrugged. 'At the confitería? You know already. It's been more of the same. Rats off a ship.'

'Onganía has brought in police from Corrientes,' he said. 'He has no authority over them, but it doesn't seem to matter. The chiefs send them anyway.'

'Do you want a glass of water?' I said.

He grunted, and I turned to pour it for him anyway. As I set it down in front of him, he rummaged in the pocket of his jacket and then casually drew out a .22 pistol and laid it on the table.

'I think you should have a gun,' he said.

For a moment I could think of nothing to say. It felt like a trick. Something to unnerve me, which I hated.

'I don't know why you don't have one already.' He examined it, as if it were a piece of jewelry he'd never seen before. 'In your line of work.'

I collected myself. 'They're difficult to travel with.'

'Well, you're not traveling now, are you?' He set the gun down on the newspaper and put a whole biscuit in his mouth. 'Foolish not to have one.'

I crossed my arms. 'This just came into your head, just now? Has something happened?'

'Things are happening all the time.'

My aunt in Nebraska had tried to teach me to shoot once, setting up a five-pound sack of flour on a fence post. I couldn't hit it. In the end she allowed me the satisfaction of murdering it in an enormous puff of white at a distance of ten feet.

'I'm not much of a marksman,' I said.

'You don't have to fire it,' Nico said. 'You just have to be willing to take it out of your pocket.'

'Is it loaded?'

'No.' He showed me, and rattled his other pocket. 'I brought you some bullets, though.' He slid the gun across the table to me. 'I look after you,' he said. He stood up, taking another biscuit, and put on his coat.

JANUARY 1958. MARYLAND YOUTH CENTER, BALTIMORE, MARYLAND

At lights out at the Maryland Youth Center I sometimes heard murmuring and cries from other rooms on the corridor in the precious thirty-minute blocks between bed checks. The matrons believed that we were delinquents because we were sluts, even those of us whose crimes weren't sexual in nature, and that we were Sapphists because we were insatiable and undiscriminating. The girls themselves seemed to feel no curiosity at all about their desire for each other; some were girlfriends, holding hands and passing notes. I missed Joanne, and this was new for me, the information that some women went to bed together habitually and casually, the same as they might do with men. Before that I could imagine sex between women only as the final calamity in a bloody drama, a self-destructive act of Hellenic proportions, Dido walking into her own funeral pyre. The world could not stand after a lesbian tryst. But it could, as it turned out, or at least it could if you had already destroyed enough of your world to be serving time in the Maryland Youth Center.

JUNE 1966. BUENOS AIRES, ARGENTINA

By the twentieth of June the senators and Perette were at their desks all day and all night, and I was keeping the same hours at my post, hunched over my equipment with a stale sandwich until four or five o'clock in the morning. To the manager in the restaurant, I delivered a long complaint about how the roof of my apartment had sprung such a bad leak in the last weeks of rain that the plaster was coming down, and while the place was being repaired I hoped I could count on his indulgence in letting me stay on a cot in the office upstairs. I offered a supplement to the rent, pretending it was from Nico. With the manager's permission I came and went whenever I liked, taking breaks only to buy empanadas and cigarettes, to use the huge white-and-gold ladies' room on the ground floor, and to stretch my legs by marching around the block in the rain. I kept the gun in a locked drawer in the desk.

The rain and the cold and the agitation in the Congreso meant that more and more business was being conducted in the confitería dining room, and during peak hours, between one o'clock and three o'clock in the afternoon, I would leave my recording equipment running in the locked room and go down to sit in a window seat with a coffee and listen.

'They're laughing at us,' said a man identified for me by the manager as the head of a barley concern out of Entre Ríos. 'They're laughing at us all over the world.' He used an elegant metaphor in which a boy with a long Beatles-style haircut he had seen waiting at a bus stop in Recoleta stood in for the ills of modern Argentina, its disregard of the church, its general hollowness and permissiveness and lack of character, all of which seemed to be enclosed within a general condition of homosexuality. Illia had been too weak to correct all this, but Onganía was strong. On the same afternoon, I listened to an assistant secretary of something – trade? internal affairs? transportation? – explain in a low voice that he had land in Uruguay and he was leaving on the ferry at the end of the week. 'They're all doing it,' he murmured to his companion, a young woman. 'All the officials, they all have summer homes and they're all going away as soon as they can.'

'But they have jobs to do,' said the woman.

'Not for very long,' he said. 'I know when I'm finished. I've already sold my wife's furniture. I won't have to come back to this fucking city for six months, and by then it will all be different.'

That Saturday was Román's birthday, and everyone was invited to gather in Victoria's apartment for liters of Quilmes beer and choripanes grilled on the racks of her oven. It was a provisional party, a weak approximation of the cookout in the country that they would have had under better circumstances, if the streets were not full of soldiers and police and every cabbie in the city weren't charging double after dark. I told her I wouldn't come because it was too dangerous, and she cursed at me over the phone, a litany of insults ending in laughter. 'Of course you will come,' she said.

'I shouldn't be out late,' I said.

'What is late? This isn't late. You are coming.'

'I can't–'

'You shouldn't hide in your flat like you do. It's bad for your health.'

It was pointless to resist her.

'Come early, if it will make you feel better,' she said.

At the last minute, as I was hunting for my shoes, I decided to take a bug with me. Perhaps this party was an opportunity.

Her apartment was at the edge of the Palermo neighborhood, on an upper floor of one of the new apartment buildings that had gone up before inflation: white, strung with balconies, ten or fifteen stories, jarring against the eroded stone and rusted ironwork that were the natural texture of the neighborhood. In the hideous mod lobby, a guard at a desk was being menaced by an enormous orange circle on the wall behind him. The building was funereally quiet, and I heard the music coming from Victoria's apartment before the doors of the elevator even opened on her floor.

Most students lived with their parents, or in grim boarding houses. Yet Victoria lived in this high-rise by herself. The grandfather with the soda factory must have been generous. I knocked softly on the door and Victoria jerked it open instantly, as if she had been waiting just inside.

'Yes, I knew it!' she said, kissing me on the cheek. 'I knew Anne was not such a coward!' Behind her, Elena was hugging her elbows and shifting her feet next to the hi-fi, and Román was trying to contain the frothing overflow of a beer bottle. He came to greet me, giving me the customary kiss on the right side of my face, with a brisk, fraternal squeeze of my shoulder at the same time, as he always did. I wished him a happy birthday, and he beamed as if I were the first person to think of this courtesy and squeezed me again, leaving a beery handprint. Elena's boyfriend, Juan José, brooded in anticipation in front of the oven, which gave out a rich smell of sausages and toasting rolls. The blue evening showed through the sliding doors of a tiny balcony, where three dark silhouettes crouched together over a joint.

'This is my bird's nest,' Victoria said, spinning in a circle. 'Very small, but just right for me.' She pressed a water glass filled with fernet and Coca-Cola into my hand and then spun away as the doorbell chimed again.

I stood in the narrow kitchen for a while with Elena, who was having some kind of problem with Juan José that I could not quite understand. His parents wanted him to leave Buenos Aires until it was safe again, and Elena thought this was cowardly but couldn't say so. The effort of not saying so was straining their relationship, making her arch and sarcastic, making him bully her in front of their friends. She held on to my forearm with one hand and a glass of beer with the other, murmuring and shaking her head, sniffling periodically, and alluding to a reservoir of shared female knowledge between us: You know how they are, how it is, they always, we always, etc. In the living room, Román was talking about the Tupamaros across the river in Uruguay, Marxists who had been robbing banks and distributing the money in the slums of Montevideo. There was a picture in a mimeographed student newspaper I'd seen of a group of young men in crew-neck sweaters, their faces covered with handkerchiefs, standing on the roof of a Peugeot, waving bricks of bundled money at an assembled crowd of old women in shawls. Román, who kept tucking an unlit cigarette behind his ear and then removing it to gesture with it, was saying that they were the real patriots, patriots of the Americas against the foreign banks. 'But they have bombs,' said someone, a girl I vaguely recognized, and he snatched the cigarette from its perch again and jabbed it toward her, triumphant, saying, 'You've been reading propaganda.' I hadn't heard him talk this way before. Perhaps, as his plans in the warehouse were developing, he was becoming more free with his ideas.

The Tupamaros were mostly college students like the people sweating and dancing in this room. They thought a revolution would be ecstatic and spontaneous. I thought they'd failed to learn the lesson of Cuba: the movie-star revolutionaries were always followed by a bleak and endless repression. The Tupamaros would make an opening with their stylish bank robberies, and the KGB would fill it. Gerry had just given me a report of KGB activity in the unions, pipe fitters bused in from remote provinces to march in protests on the Plaza de Mayo, men who had never seen a subway car who were mysteriously being put up in fine hotels. More brazen were pamphlets I'd seen denouncing United Fruit plastered to wet sidewalks just the week before, credited to youth coordinating committees that stopped just short of signing off with a red star. I thought of Castro and his four-hour state-sponsored Russian ballets, with party officials struggling not to fall asleep in the balconies lest they bring suspicion on their commitment to the revolution. That was the future that the Tupamaros would create by accident. They wanted rock and roll, and instead they would get the First People's State Theater for Opera and Ballet.

Someone turned up the hi-fi so loud that threatening static began crackling in the speakers, but Victoria didn't care. She had put red scarves over her lamps, and the living room was bathed in bordello light. Twenty or thirty people were crammed into the small apartment now. Sometime around midnight, as I was pulled into a knot of dancers hemmed in by a teetering floor lamp and a chaise longue, it dawned on me that I hadn't been to a party in at least a year.

'Victoria,' I said breathlessly, 'aren't you worried the neighbors will hear?'

'There are no neighbors,' she said. 'The building is half-empty. They haven't sold an apartment here in two years.'

I kicked off my shoes. Shoes were littered around the living room, peeping out from under the furniture like Easter eggs. Victoria clapped and spun me in a circle. I was a little drunk; I had always liked to dance. I was sweating, and the green linen dress I had chosen was sticking to my back. I remembered crashing a party in Morningside Heights full of Columbia students – that was the last time I had danced this much.

Someone had opened a bottle of champagne, and I was giddy. I went into the bathroom, a strange narrow closet with tiles in a vibrating pattern of yellow and green, to wash my hands and splash some water on my face. A dark, flushed girl looked back out of the mirror. My hair was damp, sticking to my temples, and my lipstick had all worn off. The bump in the bridge of my nose was shiny with sweat. I edged back into the hallway.

Victoria was there, holding a lit cigarette. I tried to pass by her, and she put a hand on my waist. 'Stay a minute and talk to me,' she said. She leaned close, wobbling a bit. 'Do you like Román?'

'Sure,' I said. 'I like Román.'

'Román and I are going to do important things. We are very strong together.'

'You seem very strong together,' I said.

'Very important things,' she whispered, leaning on me. 'We have big spirits. Huge spirits. Together. For the people.'

I laughed, and she laughed too. She had put most of her weight on me, the end of her cigarette was smoldering a little too close to my face, and now she squeezed my waist through the damp linen and looked frankly down my dress. She kissed me, quickly before I could pull away, and bit my lip.

'You're drunk,' I said, stepping back, shocked that she had the nerve. 'Why did you – why did you think–?' I couldn't come up with the things that a more innocent woman would say. I was surprised, but in the wrong way. Afraid that she had seen something in me. She had a greedy look on her face, her teeth showing insolently. 'Anyone could see you,' I said finally.

'See what?' she said. Her hand was on my leg.

I stepped out of range. She laughed at me. When girls like her did this in bars, they were usually more kittenish. She wasn't coy. She was flushed and amused. She swayed back toward her living room.

I was alone in the hallway, facing a framed poster from a Brecht festival in São Paulo. My mind cleared; I was nearly sober, and my hands were shaking. I took the bug from my pocket and slipped it into the back of the frame. The music from the hi-fi now sounded clattering and strange.

I stepped back into the living room, smoothing my hair with both hands. Victoria was laughing with some boys from the law school, her back to me. I drifted numbly to the balcony, where Elena was standing with a cigarette. There was a buzzing in my lip where I had been bitten.

'There you are. I was just thinking that I've been talking all night about me,' Elena said, with a sad smile. 'You always listen.'

I looked down at the street, the blue-white glow of a city bus

114

many stories below. I patted her arm. 'That's what friends are for,' I said.

I said my goodbyes soon after and left. While I walked through the hushed streets, I went over those few seconds in the hallway again and again, every step of our choreography, and decided I had done well: I had given nothing away. I had pulled back. I had shown surprise, the way most women would. Her smell was still with me – her hair, the gin on her breath.

JANUARY 1958. MARYLAND YOUTH CENTER, BALTIMORE, MARYLAND

Two weeks after Christmas, a social worker came into the dayroom looking for me and said I would be released in three days. I was being transferred to the custody of a boarding school in Delaware called the Barrington School. When she had gone, the sulky girl sitting next to me said, 'It must be nice to have money.'

'Why?' I said. 'What's the Barrington School?'

'It's where they send mental patients and sluts from nice families.'

My mother had sent a package with some of my clothes in it, my coat and heaviest sweaters, a few blouses and skirts. The package obviated any need for me to visit Chevy Chase before my move to Barrington, although there were other things I missed from my old room: books, a coverlet, my makeup box. I decided not to ask her for them. It would have afforded her a chance to be decent by sending them, and I didn't want to give her that.

They came for me at breakfast to go to Barrington. I was sitting next to my roommate, who was eating an egg and tearing her toast into bits and soliloquizing about a piece of beef that her brother had saved especially for himself once and how she had stolen it and seared it in butter and eaten it in a shed. When the social worker came through the doorway and nodded to me I said, 'Claire, I think I'm going now,' but she didn't pay any attention. I glanced back as I was leaving the room and saw her tipping the eggs and toast from my plate onto hers.

I stripped off the smock and stockings in the small room again, unobserved this time, and put on new clothes from the package. Outside it was a blinding, cold day, a light snow crusted over the grass. In the parking lot there was a blue van with 'Barrington' printed on the door. I felt free, actually, walking across the parking lot to the van, which is a funny thing. I'm sure I was smiling.

JUNE 1966. BUENOS AIRES, ARGENTINA

For two days, when I tuned in to the bug in the warehouse in La Boca, I heard nothing but an empty hiss. On the third day, the murmur of male voices. I heard snatches of their conversation through the afternoon.

'It won't be ready in time,' said a voice I didn't recognize.

'It will be ready,' said Román. He had a lilting intonation that I recognized easily. How much did he know, I wondered, about his girl? I kept turning it over in my mind. He had been just around the corner, at that party. What secrets did she allow him, if she took liberties like that?

'Carajo, this is a disaster,' said the first voice. 'We have to start over.'

And then silence, mixed with scraping sounds, footsteps. An afternoon passed that way, with unclassifiable noises and bits of conversation about the facultad.

Gerry was impatient. 'They haven't said where they'll put it, when, nothing?'

'No.'

'They must be waiting for Onganía to move.'

'Maybe. Sounds like they're having trouble with the material.'

'Keep listening.'

When the warehouse was empty, when Perette's office contained only secretaries, I listened to Victoria's apartment. In this way I learned that she had a Vandellas record that she listened to over and over again, that her mother called her every afternoon at two o'clock and asked her if she was studying, and that Román often visited during the siesta. I overheard sex one afternoon; they must have been on the living room sofa. I heard them fighting. Between them I heard the same vague anxieties that were spoken in the warehouse.

'How much longer?' Victoria said.

'Hard to say. Not much.'

'There aren't many chances.'

'Sweetheart, I know. We won't fail.'

This pretty girl, collaborating in a bombing plot. If I hadn't heard it all with my own ears, seen the equipment in La Boca with my own eyes, I would not have believed it. I understood more easily now the grim edge to Gerry's suave manner, the tense way he went through the world, enumerating dangers. The KGB was like a poison gas. It rattled me to know that it could wreak such awful havoc among bright and charming young people with the whole world to lose.

'Keep listening,' Gerry said.

It wasn't tanks but trucks that woke me from a light sleep around five o'clock on the morning of June 28. They were downshifting roughly on the street outside the confitería, one after another making the turn from Calle Rodríguez Peña onto Avenida Rivadavia. It wasn't until I had pulled a sweater on and lifted the sash to look out the window that I realized all other traffic noises had stopped. The trucks – square, flat-topped vehicles whose color I couldn't distinguish in the distorting yellow of the streetlights – were alone in the street. All other traffic had been shut down. The first in line turned left, mounted the sidewalk with a drunken-sailor lurch, and drove straight into the plaza, over the sand that was populated in the daytime by darting dogs and children. The rest of the line followed. In a moment they were assembled behind the huge dry fountain, facing the Congreso building across the empty street.

I turned on my radio, instantly wide awake. It took me a minute and a half to find the right frequency and aim the transceiver properly. When I found the signal from Perette's office, I heard the gentle, sleepy static of an empty room. Over that, faintly, I heard an echo of the trucks.

I pulled on my shoes and coat. It was still very dark in the hallway, but I left the lights off, creeping down with one hand on the wall instead. The walls were unfinished in the upper floors of the confitería, a rough lath that had never been painted, and I scraped my palm on a staple halfway down. One floor above the dining room, near the manager's office and the storerooms, I saw a light on and went toward it. It was coming from a room beside the service stairs. Leaning against a counter beside a pile of folded cloth napkins, the bag from the laundry at his feet, was the boy who'd surprised me in the top room months before. He was smoking and looking out the window at the trucks on the plaza.

He looked over his shoulder at me. 'What's happening?' he said. He gave no sign of remembering me.

'You don't know?' I said.

He shook his head. 'They're driving on the plaza,' he said. 'They're not allowed to do that.'

'It's the army,' I said. And then I said the word for coup, which in Spanish, as in French, means a strike or shock, a blow with the fist. I knocked my fist into my palm as I said it, and it stung where I'd scraped it on the stairs.

'How do you know it's a coup?' he said.

'Everybody knows,' I said. 'It's been in the papers.' I crowded in next to him to look out the window. From this lower vantage point, a couple of magnolia trees obscured part of the Congreso building, but I could still see the row of trucks idling on the sand with plumes of exhaust lit pink by their taillights. Onganía wouldn't be here; he would be at the presidential palace in the Plaza de Mayo, a mile off. It would all be timed to happen simultaneously – the trucks here at the Congreso, another contingent there at the palace. I needed to hurry. This would be my last report.

I went down to the ground floor. The vast dining room was silent and abandoned, the heat and clatter of the early-morning kitchen shift barely discernible at the far end. The loading doors were open to receive the shipment of fruit that would come at five, and two dogs in the alley behind the confitería lifted their heads as I jumped down and walked toward the streetlights still shining on Calle Rodríguez Peña. I headed east, toward the lightening gray over the river.

My route was along Avenida Rivadavia, the long artery that divided the north of the city from the south. I tried to light a cigarette without slowing down, blocking the breeze with the collar of my coat, not wanting to look too hurried but not wanting to go too slowly either. Newspapers were being delivered to the kiosk at the corner of Uruguay, and the deliveryman and the proprietor were chatting over the bundles with their hands in their pockets, looking toward the plaza behind me, which was mostly obscured now by Beaux-Arts

121

apartment buildings. The rumble of trucks was faint already, even just a few blocks away.

Before Avenida 9 de Julio I passed a nightclub with the doors propped open, young people streaming out into the street. I was startled by the intrusion of raucous night-time into this quiet dawn moment. It was morning and maneuvers were underway, but they didn't know. The nightclub was called Le Troc. Through the open doorway I heard the Kinks, or something like the Kinks. A drunk girl, young enough that her weaving across the sidewalk seemed lamblike and sweet, stopped in front of me and took the cigarette from her lips. She started to sing in a cartoonish growl. 'Giiiiirl,' she sang, and then a run of slurred nonsense, the lyrics from 'You Really Got Me.' I was hypnotized by her for a moment and then hurried away.

By the time I turned onto Calle Florida the streets were filled with trucks and soldiers, and four polite young cadets told me the Plaza de Mayo was closed. The light from the streetlamps was beginning to look weak: the sun was coming up. At the corner of Avenida Sarmiento, a few blocks from the Plaza de Mayo, I came across a cadet in a blue helmet smoking a cigarette in the lee of a bank.

'What's happening on the plaza?' I said.

He started as if he wasn't supposed to be there, too far from his fellows, away from the action. 'Who are you?' he said.

'What's happening on the plaza?' I said again.

He glanced in that direction and dropped the cigarette. 'The generals,' he said.

'Which generals?'

'Onganía. Of course.' He laughed. 'Are you a student? A tourist?'

In the distance I could hear a loudspeaker, but couldn't make out the words. The cadet was hugging himself against the chill morning. 'He's all right, the old man,' he said, meaning Illia, I guessed. 'But he's not doing us any good.' A low rumble reached our ears, a wash of mechanical knocking and grinding over a thrum of combustion, and a tank came into view around the corner of Avenida Maipú. The soldier and I both stepped back as it blustered our way. For an instant it was like a wall in front of us, vibrating and hot, and then it was shrinking away down the middle of the empty avenue, trailing blue exhaust.

I needed to get my things – everything, all the equipment out of the confitería first of all, and then whatever I could strip out of the flat in San Telmo. And then I had to get to the ferry launch on the river and book a ticket to Uruguay. I could be in Montevideo by nightfall if I hurried. I had planned for this, but I felt a trace of nausea, a buzz in my extremities and heaviness in my stomach, like stage fright.

The cadet was still staring after the tank. 'I wish I had a camera,' he said.

I went back to the confitería first. It hadn't opened at the usual time, which was six o'clock. When I approached from the front I saw first the strange deadness of the front windows, dark and empty, and then a few policemen standing in a casual group on the corner. I doubled back two blocks and approached again from the rear, hurrying through the back alley, which was divested now even of its dogs, and let myself in by the service entrance with the key the manager had given me.

The place was deserted. The great ringing kitchen was empty. Behind the bar, a row of demitasses stretched infinitely in the dim light from the street. I went up the back stairs, taking them two at a time, so that I was coughing by the time I reached the office. I packed up all the recording equipment into a green leather case. I swept the crust of a sandwich and an empty Coke bottle into a paper bag, folded up the cot I had been sleeping on and propped it against the wall, and put my sachet of toiletries, my toothbrush and powder case and throat lozenges, into my handbag. I was on the landing, struggling to close the door behind me with both hands full, when I remembered the loaded gun that I had locked away in the desk drawer weeks before. I emptied the chamber and put the gun in my coat pocket.

I waited ten minutes for the bus, realized finally that it would never come, and hailed a taxi. The driver seemed excited. He kept looking in the rear-view mirror at me, and as we waited at a red light at a deserted intersection – uncharacteristic of a Buenos Aires cabdriver – he turned up the radio and I heard the first official report of the morning.

'Dr. Illia has left the presidential palace,' said the newscaster, over a penetrating low whine. 'General Onganía will make a statement shortly.'

The cabdriver was chewing on his thumbnail. A bunch of dried flowers hung from the rear-view mirror, trembling with the idling engine. He swiveled in his seat.

'Can you believe this bullshit?' he said.

'It's an outrage,' I said.

'It's a fucking outrage,' he said, facing forward again. 'She knows,' he added, jerking his thumb at me, as if for the benefit of an audience.

In his distraction he turned the wrong way down one of the one-way streets that stymied the flow of traffic around my apartment building, and started cursing and hauling on the wheel. 'Here is fine,' I said, grossly overtipping him, and hefted my things out onto the sidewalk. I could still hear him grinding gears, reversing in fractions in the narrow street, as I walked the last block home, the green case knocking against my legs. A cold drizzle had started up again. The street was deserted. As I passed the café on the corner where I sometimes sat with the newspaper, I heard a radio. Inside I could see an old waiter standing behind the counter with his arms folded, listening to the portable wireless that I sometimes heard emitting the distant roar of a soccer game on Sundays, now tuned to the news and playing at full volume to the empty dining room. 'The generals will make a statement.'

At the building beside mine, two boys in primary school uniforms were sitting on the step.

'Is there no school today?' I said.

'Mama said no,' answered the bigger boy.

'We're going to go to the park,' said the little one. 'When the rain stops.'

'We're not allowed to go to the park,' the older one said, exasperated, as if he'd been saying it all morning. 'It's dangerous at the park today.'

'Mama said we could go to the park,' wailed the little one.

'She said another day,' said the older one. 'You don't listen!'

Upstairs, I started in the bedroom, pulling my dresses out of the closet. A box under the window held receipts and grocery lists, pamphlets from museums I had visited on lonely days, my library card, a stack of magazines. I sifted out a few things that had my handwriting on them, took them to the kitchen, opened the window, and burned them in the sink. Then I rinsed the ashes down the drain.

Nico would understand why I had gone; there was no need to contact him.

I thought of Victoria and Román.

I felt tired, suddenly, and bent down to rest my elbows on the edge of the sink. I thought of Victoria and felt relief that I would soon be away from her, her flamboyance, her unpredictable movements, her indiscretion. I lit a cigarette. But there was something else as well, under the relief.

I flipped on the television in the living room. One station played a test pattern. Another was dark static, with snowy figures moving in it. The third showed a newscaster sitting at a desk, waiting for a cue that didn't come, his arms limp at his sides.

Victoria's attention had been like a spotlight on me – blinding, acute – and soon it would be gone. I would be back in the States in a few days or weeks, and I would never know what she had wanted from me.

I hesitated beside the telephone, scolded myself out of the impulse, and went back to the bedroom to pack my shoes and stockings and my good coat. A moment later, the telephone rang. I hurried back out of the bedroom.

'Hello?' I said.

'So you're at home,' Nico said.

'Is everything all right?' I said, hoping that he could divine the questions nested within the question.

'Yes, it's fine, all fine,' he said. 'You're not in your perch today?'

'Of course not,' I said shortly. I was confused by Nico's openness on this unsecured line. Maybe it was despair. He had said before that he hated every coup, although his boss would be happy with Onganía. Or perhaps he was drunk. Late at night when I couldn't sleep, those last few weeks before the coup, I had seen men leaving the bar on the corner at last call, half-buttoned into their jackets, lurching alone down the sidewalks in the cold. I wondered if that was how Nico had been passing his time. In a bar in Barracas, maybe, until late at night, complaining to neighbors who wouldn't repeat what he said, and then home again to his sleeping wife, bringing the cold in his coat and hair.

'So you are abandoning us,' he murmured. 'I think you ought to stay. Safer to stay, really, for a week or two.'

I didn't like the soft voice he was using. 'Are you drunk?' I glanced at the clock: it was eight o'clock in the morning.

'I wanted to know if you'd spoken to your man at the CIA,' he said.

I was so angry for a moment that I pressed the receiver to my chest. I blinked for a few seconds, staring at the heavy curtains drawn across the French doors to the balcony, and then lifted the receiver again and said, 'What man?'

He laughed. 'What man.'

'How does your wife feel about these calls?' I said, and hung up.

The buzzing in my palms and the soles of my feet was becoming unpleasant. If the phone rang again, I wouldn't answer it. I stepped out onto the balcony to finish the cigarette, even though it was cold and I was wearing house slippers. A low winter sun shone over the buildings across the street, picking out the television aerials and whitewashed chimneys. At the corner of Humberto Primo two olive-drab trucks roared by, soldiers standing in the beds like cattle, miserable in the cold. A traffic cop saluted as they passed.

Goodbye, Buenos Aires, I thought. Then I said it out loud. I felt more remote in Buenos Aires than I ever had, and maybe that was close to happiness, being adrift far down the Atlantic coast with thousands of miles of grasslands at my back, the south a desert that stretched to the Antarctic Circle, even the river an empty expanse, the far shore never visible.

I checked twice to be sure the gas was off on the stove and the water heater, and then I went out, carrying two cases, all I had. I took the key with me. I wondered how long it would take the landlord to notice I had gone.

JUNE 1959. THE BARRINGTON SCHOOL, MIDDLETOWN, DELAWARE / NEW YORK, NEW YORK

My mother sent me a letter the month before graduation, explaining that she had received an invitation to commencement from the school, but because it was so painful for her to see the mess I had made of my life, she would be in the Virgin Islands instead. I spent an afternoon sunbathing on a weedy Chesapeake beach rather than attend the ceremony, which was thronged with the disappointed parents of the delinquent senior class.

Afterward, at a loss for anything else to do, I went up to New York on the train with a cardboard suitcase and my best friend from the dorm, a girl named Cathy who wanted to be an actress. We moved into a boarding house and found jobs as waitresses in a cocktail bar with pretensions on the west side. I couldn't stand the job for long. After a few months I left for work as a typist with Consolidated Edison, which was so boring that once, around two o'clock in the afternoon, I suffered a hallucination in which the periods and commas on the notice in my typewriter began to pulsate gently on the page. A few weeks later I went out for lunch and never came back.

JUNE 1966. BUENOS AIRES, ARGENTINA

The cabs didn't want to stop. I waited for twenty minutes on the Avenida Independencia as they went by, conspicuous in a green raincoat with my bags, visibly foreign and outbound, beginning to sweat under my collar despite the cold. Soldiers appraised me from trucks. If they stopped me I would pretend to be rich and naïve. I had thousands in cash in my purse. There was a way of offering a bribe that made you look like you didn't even realize what you were doing. Two more cabs sailed by in tandem, two more drivers not even glancing toward the sidewalk.

Puerto Madero was only a mile and a half away, but the walk would take thirty minutes, and with my bags I would be obvious to every policeman and soldier I passed. I could abandon one case here if I needed to, on the sidewalk – it contained only clothes – but the other held my equipment and would have to either come with me or be dropped into the canal that separated the city proper from the spiky, chaotic fringe of the port. Just then a cab turned the corner onto Independencia and was stopped short by the wheezing passage of an empty bus, and while the driver was still cursing and banging on the horn I jerked open the back door and threw my bags onto the seat.

'I'm not taking anybody! I'm not taking anybody!' he yelled. I slammed the door shut behind me. 'Fifty pesos for Puerto Madero,' I said.

'Nobody!' he said.

'Are you out of your mind? Fifty pesos!' I said.

'Eighty pesos!' he said. 'I don't know who you are!'

I gestured my submission to this, slumping down in the seat, and he pulled into traffic. A lot of cabbies between San Telmo and the river would be going home rich tonight. When Castro came to Havana, the old plantation families thronged the airport depots along the northern coast of the island with cash and jewelry and even their best furniture, loaded into borrowed farm trucks. The bush pilots of Cuba became kings overnight. Their wives wore pearls for months.

We crossed the Avenida Paseo Colón at a hysterical pace, and then edged onto the bridge over the canal. Traffic was heavy here. Through a gap in the warehouses along the docks I could see the river, placid and brown in this season from the rain falling hundreds of miles north in Misiones, no waves and no glint of sun, no other shore, a view like the unfinished edge of a drawing. Then we were over the bridge and past the customs buildings, and the driver jerked to a stop in front of the ferry terminal, which was swarmed with cabs.

'Quickly,' he said. 'I want to go home.'

I paid him and picked my way through a triple ring of cabs that were circling and jockeying for space at the curb. Women with undone faces chaperoned anxious children. Men were lined up five and ten deep at the pay phones. University professors and union men, I guessed, the leftist middle class. I hoped they had Uruguayan relatives to visit, that none of this would go down too badly. I had the nervous guilt of a survivor already as

132

I smoked a last cigarette by the heavy doors.

The line for the ticket counter was long, stretching down one side of the terminal toward the shuttered café at the far end. I waited thirty minutes for my turn. The man at the ticket desk, when I finally reached him, was red-faced despite the cold morning, sitting on a high stool beside a ticket-printing machine, with a radio at his elbow droning a constant promise of more news soon to come.

'Destination?' he said.

'Montevideo.'

'Round trip?'

'One way.'

'Passport,' he said.

I slid it across the desk and began to dig in my bag for the money.

'Canadian,' he said.

I glanced up at him with a polite smile, both hands still on my pocketbook. 'Yes,' I said.

'You are aware of what happened this morning?'

My eyes went to the radio. 'Yes, of course,' I said.

'Foreigners are not traveling out of Argentine ports today,' he said.

I began to sweat. I felt myself circling over a deep emptiness, like a bird above a canyon.

'I don't really understand what you mean,' I said, broadening my accent. 'My Spanish is–' I shrugged apologetically. 'I have to go to Montevideo. A friend is expecting me.'

'No movement of foreigners,' he said.

'But it's all arranged.'

'It is not arranged,' he said. He had put one foot down on the floor and was now half-standing, half-leaning on the high stool.

'It is not possible.'

'I don't understand,' I tried again.

He looked at me with frank hatred. 'There is no movement of foreigners today,' he said again, pushing the passport away as if it were filthy. 'These are orders from the police. You are delaying the line.'

'I'll buy a return ticket if that's what you want,' I said. 'With cash.' A bribe.

'You are delaying the line,' he said again.

'I have enough,' I said, holding up my wallet, but the gesture was too obvious and I saw his face crumple in disgust. The muttering of the people behind me had stopped, and I could feel eyes on my back.

'I will call the police,' he said.

We stared at each other for a moment. 'I'm going to speak to the embassy,' I said, only because it was the kind of thing a person with a real passport would say. I made for the nearest doors, which opened onto the pier.

The cold air was a relief. Behind me, the terminal was a seething mass of people, but the narrow pier was empty. I took off my hat. I'd gotten hot, my nerve failing. I thought hard for a minute, looking down into the brown water rising and falling below the tarred pilings, and then emptied my second suitcase over the edge of the boards. My recording equipment disappeared into the water. A seagull the size of a chicken landed on the railing and screeched. I walked the long way around the terminal, leaving the empty suitcase in a garbage bin, and headed back toward my apartment, the mile and a half that I had just covered at such exorbitant cost.

When I stepped onto the landing on my floor, the door of my apartment was open. I had not left it open. I remembered turning the key in the lock. I could feel my pulse in my temples and ears. From downstairs, faintly, I could hear the barking of the Pomeranian in the apartment of the optometrist and his wife. I edged to the right so I could see through the open doorway and into the living room beyond.

The damask sofa had been pulled away from the far wall, and the fabric across the back of it had been cut away from the frame so it trailed on the floor in long strips. It had a dazed, pretty air, like a girl in a ruined dress. The lamb painting lay face down in its frame on the parquet.

I was back down the stairs and halfway down the block before I realized what I was doing. It was only when I stopped to catch my breath beside a newspaper stand that I remembered I was carrying a gun in my shoulder bag. If I had wondered whether I was the type of woman who would confront a stranger with a gun, I was now relieved of any uncertainty. I was not the type. Had there been anyone in the apartment as I stood in the hallway?

I walked for a while and then started to feel weak in the legs. I went into a bar that was open and asked for a glass of whiskey and drank it on a stool in the corner. The radio was on, still promising more news soon.

There had probably been no one in the apartment when I was standing in the hallway. No one would ransack an apartment with the door open. So whoever had done it had been fast and timed it well – come and gone in the hour I had been away.

I remembered Nico, that strange drunken call just before I left for the ferry. Advising me against Montevideo. Wheedling with me to stay. I had been betrayed.

I stared into the mirror above the bar. Inviting me up for dinner with his wife. She knows a liar when she sees one.

After a few minutes I returned to myself, noticed what I looked like, smoothed my hair. My hands were shaking.

What would he gain from giving me up, from having the police turn over my apartment?

The tremble had gone out of my legs, but I still felt weak and I would need to find someplace to hide. The barman whistled to himself, a moody little milonga, casting sideways glances at me. 'What kind of day is this,' he said to the empty bar, to me. 'What a shame.'

I nodded and said nothing.

'It's a shock to the nerves,' he said. 'Another drink?'

'No, thank you.'

'Where are you from, miss?'

'France.'

'Beautiful country.'

I dropped my money on the bar and slipped back out onto the sidewalk. A light, cold rain had begun to fall again. It seemed like the street and sky were darkening, as if a drawstring were being pulled shut overhead. I didn't know how much Nico knew about me or my movements or connections in Buenos Aires. The man he had following me might know about Victoria and Elena and Román and their friends, because I saw them often. I couldn't run safely in their direction.

I considered hotels. I was standing in the rain now, facing a tattered park across the street, my view interrupted every so often by a cab with its lights switched off. Any foreigner checking into a hotel would be a cause for suspicion on a day like today. The Argentines were always alert to signs of foreign interference in their politics. Some would be theorizing already that the Americans, so enamored of Onganía, were behind what had happened this morning.

Perhaps that was why Nico wanted to feed me to the police: to bolster this impression, which would cast suspicion on Onganía. I would have bet a thousand dollars that at that moment while I stood getting steadily more damp and more anxious on a sidewalk in San Telmo, the Buenos Aires police were tearing apart the attic room in the Confitería del Molino. I needed to get off the street immediately.

An orange cat looked balefully at me from under a parked Citroën.

I thought of James, the mod I had met that night in the bar. I remembered his apartment, which faced a large French-style building across Calle Riobamba that looked like a nunnery in the dark. I couldn't remember the number of his building, but I was almost sure it was on the corner of Tucumán. And the longer I stood and looked at the ragged orange cat and felt the chill coming through my coat, the more it seemed clear that he was the only person I knew in Buenos Aires whom I could be sure Nico knew nothing about.

DECEMBER 1959. GREENWICH VILLAGE, NEW YORK CITY

It was around the time I quit my job as a typist with Con Edison that I finally worked up the courage to go into the Bracken. The Bracken was a piano bar in the Village that I had heard of, by reputation, from other girls at the boarding house; they were making fun of a new arrival from Texas, who had been going down there to cadge drinks and plates of spaghetti from the dykes who worked for the transit authority. Like many things at the boarding house, the Bracken was at once a place that everybody knew about and that nobody would admit to having been to. Twice I walked past the narrow door without going in, and once I hesitated for a few minutes at the end of the block, pretending to be waiting for a bus. I saw women go in and out – some with lipstick on, hair curled and pinned, and some who wore big black shoes and kept their cigarettes tucked behind their ears. I saw a few men, too, laughing and joking with their arms around each other.

I had no one to go with me. I couldn't ask Cathy. I had gone with girls at the Barrington School, but that place was a cloister, where the girls romanced each other out of boredom and loneliness as much as real desire. A running joke in the senior class compared these relationships to the arrangements made by men trapped on ships on long ocean voyages. This was different. I was out in the world and I couldn't pretend it was a game anymore. I could have a good time with men, but with women it was different: I was lit up, rattled, consumed.

I chose an evening when Cathy was out on a date with a law student and dressed carefully in our room. I chose a shift that I thought was very chic – it was black and it did something clever with the draping on one shoulder but otherwise refused to call attention to itself, and it made me feel a bit like a French girl, or at least a co-ed at the New School. I looked nice, I thought. I was tall, and my legs were all right.

The Bracken was crowded and noisy, a fog of smoke around half-lit chandeliers. Colored Moroccan lanterns hung over the bar; the banquettes were draped in old velvet, and the wood floor showed through in places where the linoleum had been danced away. I pushed my way to the bar, licking dry lips. A woman whose short hair was combed back with oil stared straight into my eyes, her expression blank, and I let my gaze drop to the floor. The barmaid brought me a gimlet and I edged onto a stool. Beside me, a row of girls in cocktail dresses clung close together, laughing, prodding at the ice in their drinks with straws.

Butch women stood in clusters at the back of the room. While I watched, one woman approached the girls to my right and pushed in deftly among them, ordering a round, dropping a white hand onto the shoulders of the smallest blonde. My drink was empty, and it was hard to catch the barmaid's eye. The blonde girl next to me, lost in her romance, laughed uproariously and elbowed me hard in the ribs, looking round a moment later with bleary eyes, as if not sure she'd made contact with a real person. 'Sorry,' she said. She studied me, her eyes narrowing, then turned pointedly away.

At that point I decided to try harder at getting drunk. I caught the arm of the barmaid as she went by, and she looked up, irritated. 'Another gimlet, please,' I said. Maybe she could see something in my face; her look softened. She mixed the drink and then stepped aside and said something to a woman with a painted-on beauty mark at the end of the bar.

Now I was drunk. The girls on my right had paired up and were dancing near the piano. The man at the keys played 'Don't Get Around Much Anymore' with a twelve-inch ivory cigarette holder clenched between his teeth. I smoked a cigarette and then another. The feeling of being invisible stopped being so awful.

When my drink was empty, I drifted unsteadily out to the sidewalk, trying and failing to button my coat. I felt a heaviness that was a step past tears.

'Are you all right?'

I lurched back and squinted. It was the woman with the beauty mark.

'Am I what?' I said, trying to be dignified.

She smirked. She was holding a thin jacket closed. The night had gotten cold. 'It's because they think you're a cop,' she said. 'That's why no one would talk to you.'

I must have looked shocked, because she laughed. 'I'm not a cop,' I said.

'You're not femme enough to be a femme and you're obviously not a butch,' she said. 'So they think you're a cop.'

My coat was hanging open. I looked down at my clothes, my shoes.

'I like your dress,' she said. 'It's not that it's not a nice dress.' She brushed a hair behind her ear. 'Are you hungry? There's a place around the corner that sells burgers.'

JUNE 1966. BUENOS AIRES, ARGENTINA

James's apartment building was larger and whiter than I remembered it, seeing it now sober and in daylight. I pressed the bell at the side of the filigreed iron gate and then realized it wasn't locked. I went in and climbed the stairs. It had been months since that night we left the bar together, but I remembered that his door was on the third floor, beside an alcove at the top of the stairs. There was a prayer placard on the door that looked like it predated the building.

'¿Quién es?' said a voice from within.

'It's Anne,' I said, and my voice came out with an exaggerated mid-Atlantic flatness, as if to brush aside his carefully accented question. 'Anne from – from a couple of months ago. From the Bar Catalán.'

There was a long, ponderous silence. I dropped my face into my hands. You are all right, you are all right, I said to myself. You are quick and smart. He will open the door. You will not go to prison today. He will open the door.

I heard footsteps within and then another long hesitation. I cleared my throat and brightened my voice. 'Maybe you don't remember me,' I said to the peephole. 'I'm sorry to come on a day like this. You must be thinking–'

The door opened and he appeared in the gap, unshaven, wearing glasses I didn't remember, in an undershirt. His hair was standing up. He looked like a cadet in a war movie, about to go into France.

'Anne?' he said.

I mustered an apologetic smile.

'I couldn't remember your name. You sneaked out,' he said. His face was open and curious, but he was not smiling.

'Can I come in, please?' I said.

He stepped back out of the doorway. The room beyond was larger than I remembered it, perhaps an effect of daylight coming through the large street-facing windows, the white bulk of the colonial building opposite, its terracotta roof leaching Mediterranean warmth into the winter day. A weaving on the living room wall showed the eagle and snake from the Mexican flag, their details picked out in pink and green thread. Between the windows there was a framed photograph of an Aztec sculpture, a pre-Columbian face laughing riotously, crowned with feathers, with a knife for a tongue.

'Well,' I said.

'Is this a social call?' he said. I watched him pick up a sweater that was draped across the back of a chair and pull it on, then resettle his glasses and run a hand over his hair. He was only slightly taller than I was, and he had a ready stance, like a boxer.

The room was neat and settled. No sign that he was packing up.

'My apartment was ransacked,' I said. 'I'm afraid to go back there.'

His eyebrows went up. 'Ransacked? By who?'

I suddenly wanted to sit down. 'I have no idea.'

'Was anything missing?'

'I was too scared to go inside. The door was open when I got there, I didn't know if they were still there.'

'Well, you have to call the police.' His arms were akimbo now, like a marionette.

I laughed. 'The police?'

He was already walking toward the phone hanging on the wall in the kitchen, but at this he stopped and turned around. 'Right, I guess this isn't the day for it. Do you think it was them that did it? I've heard of that happening. People get home and there's a note on the door telling them to come in for questioning and all the cash in the place is gone.'

I pretended to consider this with dawning horror. 'I guess it could have been.'

'Sit down,' he said. I sat in the chair under the eagle and snake. He rattled in the kitchen for a few moments and then came out with a cup of instant coffee that he handed to me. 'You're a student?'

'Yes. Psychology at the UC.'

'Maybe they're cracking down on students. They're always suspicious of psychologists anyway. All those dirty books.'

This was true. There was an antipathy between Freudians and political conservatives in Argentina that had persisted for decades. If James was willing to make this argument for me, I would let him. 'But I'm not even Argentine.'

'Well, that's even worse. A foreign psychology student. They probably think you're transmitting straight to Moscow.'

I laughed uproariously.

'Has anybody been after you at the university?' he said.

'Oh, I don't know. I don't think so.' I drank some of the foamy coffee. My hands were still unsteady. 'I tried to go to Montevideo this morning, just until things settle down, and they wouldn't sell me a ticket at Puerto Madero. They said there are no foreign passports going in or out today. And then I went back to my apartment and it was – well, I told you. And now here I am.'

'You don't have friends here?'

'No. I haven't been here long. Just a few months.'

'I thought you said you'd arrived just after New Year's.' Something changed in his tone, as if he had caught me in a lie. A black cat appeared from under the sofa and rubbed against my leg.

'Six months, then,' I said.

'Six months and all alone. You seem awfully friendly for that.'

I glanced up. His arms were folded.

'I'm pretty shy, really,' I said.

He was avoiding my eyes. 'I'm surprised you remembered this place,' he said. 'To find your way back.'

'I've got a good memory,' I said. Was he angry with me? That happened sometimes. They got angry with you for being too easy, for going on existing afterward. The Aztec sculpture in the photo stared me down.

James got up abruptly and looked out the window. 'More trucks,' he said, over the diesel squalling in the street.

There was a long silence.

'It's just very unexpected,' he said finally.

'You're right. I shouldn't have come,' I said. I set the coffee cup down on a magazine, relieved to get rid of it, the caffeine mixing badly with my adrenaline. I stood up, red-faced. 'I'm so sorry. I'll try the airport. Maybe I'll be luckier there. I've got some money.'

'No, no. You don't have to–'

'It's all right.' I picked my handbag up off the floor and the

145

cat struck at the scarf trailing from it, pulling it off in a long smooth sweep to the floor. 'I just – it's all right.'

'It could be dangerous.' He was distressed now, hands open. I tried to disentangle the cat's paws from the scarf, but she was rolling silkily on the rug now, delighted.

'I'll be fine,' I said.

'You won't be. You know that. You hear the same things I do.' He meant the secret jails, the beatings. 'Stay here.'

I gave up on the scarf and straightened up, letting him see my reddened eyes, then pressed my hands to my face.

'I can't,' I said.

'Of course you can, it's easy.' He took the handbag from my arm and set it down on the table. 'I'll make you something to eat. I feel badly now, I upset you. And you had such a bad morning already. Do you want to lie down?'

I realized then how long I had been awake already that day. He pointed me toward the bedroom and I lay for a while in the aquatic dimness of the bed I barely remembered, the windows heavily curtained to keep out the light. I slept and had a dream that I was in the basket of a hot-air balloon that was rising and rising through thinning air, the sky shining on all sides, the earth becoming illegible in the distance. I woke with an ache in my chest and heard the subsiding whistle of a teakettle in the kitchen. I read the spines of the paperbacks on the night table: Graham Greene, Patricia Highsmith. Novels about liars. I needed to call Gerry.

If I could get back to America I would cash out everything and buy a house on a river and train up a big vicious dog that loved only me. A house and a dog. A trellis with some clematis on it. I ached and there was shame somewhere in it, for wandering so far away, for being so unconnected, about to be twenty-six years old with no one in the world wishing me well, no one who knew anything about me that was true at least, only this man in the other room, whose ego couldn't bear the thought of sending me away to be arrested and tortured in the sub-basement of some police station in Avellaneda, as had happened to others before and would happen again.

He tapped on the door and pushed it open a crack. 'I warmed up some empanadas,' he said. 'And soup. Campbell's. Did you know they sell it here?'

'I didn't,' I said.

The afternoon was growing dim already, steel gray through the living room windows. My mind was clearer now than it had been before. He had set out the food on a small table with flowers carved around the edge, the kind of thing a proper señora would keep polished with wax. The radio was on. The government was now headed by a junta of three, whose names I had heard from time to time in the confitería. But where was Onganía in all this?

'You have nice furniture,' I said. In a half-silvered mirror I caught my reflection before I sat down: my skirt crushed, with concentric creases radiating from my hips, and my hair a mass aggravated by sleep and humidity, impenetrable and black.

'The apartment came furnished,' he said. 'But the art is mine.'

I looked again at the eagle and snake. The snake's body was caught in one talon and it curved back on itself as if about to strike, the tongue a furious neon pink.

'That snake looks like he might make it,' I said.

James was not listening. The radio was making the trilling noise that meant there was a bulletin. 'All officeholders are relieved of their duties.'

'All of them?' James said, mostly to himself.

'All services are suspended. Curfew in effect from sunset to sunrise.'

'You couldn't have gone anywhere anyway,' he observed to me, and then added, as if to clarify, 'They said there's a curfew. Can you speak Spanish?'

So this had not been clear from our night in the bar. I wondered how much he remembered. 'Yes,' I said.

'I'm sorry to leave it on while we're eating. I don't want to miss anything.'

'I don't mind.'

The radio went into a patriotic fugue state. A person of indeterminate gender with a dry, tremulous voice read aloud from Martín Fierro, a poem about horses and knives, with breaks for 'Ave Maria' and the national anthem, sung by a soprano over a remote and crackling orchestra.

'You're Mexican?' I said finally.

'My parents came from Oaxaca to Texas before I was born,' he said. 'We used to spend summers there. My grandfather was a senator.'

The empanada was so good that my hunger came back all at once, almost painfully. I took another from the plate he had left in the middle of the table. A warm smell of cumin rose from it when I broke it in half.

'Do you think the markets will be open tomorrow?' I said. 'I don't want to eat up all your food.'

'I don't know. This is my first coup.'

'Ha. Mine too.'

I ate my soup very slowly, in shallow spoonfuls. James had forgotten half his food on his plate.

'Do you mind if I smoke?' he said. 'It's just nerves.'

'Go ahead.'

'Tell me again where you're from,' he said.

'Toronto,' I said.

'Oh, yes. You said.'

'What do you do, James?'

'I'm in the family business. Leather imports. But actually – well, I'm AWOL from the family business, if you want to know the truth. I was supposed to go back last year. But I had a crisis, I guess.'

'A crisis?'

'Couldn't face it. Going back to Houston, managing the warehouses. So I stayed here. I told them I was researching new techniques. Cutting-edge stuff in the tanneries in Corrientes. And I was for a while. But then that was all done and I still couldn't face going back.'

'And now here you are,' I said.

'Here I am. A cosmic irony. I didn't want to leave and now I can't.'

'You're attached.'

'Can't help it,' he said.

The curfew announcement came on again. He wasn't looking at me much, and his body was hunched sideways at the table, one arm braced across his stomach as he listened to the radio. Maybe he felt me watching him. He glanced up.

'I'm not an idiot,' he said.

I teetered. 'What?'

'Who was it who turned your apartment over? It was a boyfriend, wasn't it?'

This was an unexpected turn. 'A boyfriend?'

'Or a husband, maybe? You come home with me and run out in the middle of the night. Three months later your apartment has been trashed and you're back here. With no connections in the world, according to you.' He gestured with the cigarette in a way that seemed self-conscious. 'If it's money you're after, don't bother,' he added, taking a drag. It occurred to me that his watch was expensive. 'I've got none left.'

Here the best path was obvious. 'I'm not after any money,' I said. 'I have money.'

'Is he Canadian as well?' James said. 'Has he run out already?'

I needed to slow it down. 'I'd rather not talk about him,' I said, experimentally.

'Should I be expecting him to show up here and murder us both?'

In this drama that James was scripting, the man I pictured – the betrayer, or the betrayed, whichever he would be, standing in the rubble of my living room, cuckolded, shouting, red in the face – was Nico. It had a dreamy logic to it. Certainly we had parted ways definitively that day.

'I don't think so,' I said. 'He wouldn't. He's married.'

'Married?' A flicker of genuine moral shock, before he remembered to be louche.

'I'm so sorry about all this,' I said.

He looked satisfied now. He settled back into his chair. 'It's all right,' he said. 'You're livening up this lockdown, anyway.'

'So sorry,' I said again. I reached out with my soup spoon and cut the last empanada in half.

After we ate, I tried to read an old mystery novel from the shelves in the living room while James smoked and listened to the radio. I couldn't fully take in either the radio broadcast or the book, which was an Agatha Christie novel set, oddly, in ancient Egypt. At eleven o'clock we were both drowsy, the nerves of the day finally overtaken by fatigue, and there was a crisis of manners.

'Take the bed,' he said.

'No, no, no,' I said.

There were sirens in the distance, rising and falling along the river. He switched the radio off. The coughing and droning of police motorcycles sounded in the street below.

'The sofa is too small,' he said.

'If it's too small for me, it'll be worse for you.'

'My mother would be appalled if I let a guest sleep on the sofa,' he said.

'My mother would be appalled about everything that's happened since I woke up this morning.'

He was hesitating in the archway that led from the living room to the kitchen. Poking around with the dishes, which I had washed. I thought maybe he expected that we would sleep together again – maybe he thought he deserved it, for being so broad-minded about me – but I also had a feeling I had better not start it myself. It would seem too transactional if I did, and that would bother him.

'The sofa is really all right,' I said. 'I'm insisting.'

'We'll renegotiate tomorrow,' he said.

DECEMBER 1959. GREENWICH VILLAGE, NEW YORK CITY

The bars were letting out, and the streets of the Village were filled with young people singing and arguing. The woman's name was Sheila. She took me to a diner on Charles Street and bought me a burger, because she felt badly about how my night had gone. The place was as bright and noisy and clean at 2:00 AM as a hospital cafeteria. Now I could see how smoothly her face was powdered, how carefully her hair was done; she was Italian, I thought, she had the richness of the Italian girls I had watched going into the parish church in Chevy Chase when I was a child. She had a silver filling I could see when she laughed, and her nails were bitten down. The doom that I had felt in the Bracken became a funny misunderstanding while I ate, an anecdote about a naïve girl I had already ceased to be. Sheila was a student at Dartmouth. She was in town for the weekend. I knew, even as she told me this, that it wasn't true; maybe it was because I had seen the way the barmaid spoke to her. She was part of this scene, I could tell, and she was older than a college student. She lied to me and flirted with me, and I finished eating and reached under the table to let my hand rest on her knee.

She took me to an apartment a few blocks away. There was a

bathtub in the kitchen; I sat on the edge of it while she mixed us both a drink, and I drank mine without pausing for a breath, I was so nervous. I could sense that other people were sleeping in the darkened rooms of the apartment, but I said nothing and she pretended we were alone.

In the dark of an untidy bedroom, she took the empty glass out of my hand and sat on the bed. Sirens were going up the avenue. 'How green are you?' she said, and I considered a few lies, but then said, 'I went to a girls' school, but we never got much time alone.' She laughed at that as if it were the funniest thing she'd ever heard, and then she bent and pulled her stockings off.

I woke early, blinking in the tiny bedroom. Drying laundry was hung over all the furniture; ropes of necklaces dangled from the lamps, and hairpins were scattered across the floor. Sheila breathed softly, facing the wall. I pulled my dress on and stepped clumsily into my shoes, and then – being a little hopeful – I left a slip of paper on the nightstand with my name and the number of the boarding house.

It was a cold morning and I walked home through empty streets, my coat half-unbuttoned. My breath plumed in front of me; my skin felt too soft, a border that could barely hold between my hot self and the freezing air. She had been avid, unembarrassed, and somehow ironic at the same time; I thought I could sense her laughing faintly at me in the dark, and yet it was not unfriendly and I accepted it. Her gestures trailed through my mind.

JUNE 1966. BUENOS AIRES, ARGENTINA

In the morning the radio said that Onganía was being sworn in as president to replace the junta of three, and James went out to get a newspaper. I needed to call Gerry, but it wasn't safe to use the phone in the apartment. I slipped out of the building, taking the extra key hanging beside the front door, and found a pay phone three blocks away. The woman at Gerry's service sounded just the same as always. It was comforting, in a remote way. I asked her to have Gerry call me back, hung up, and stood shivering next to the phone box. It rang almost immediately.

'When are you coming back?' Gerry said. 'I thought you'd be in Montevideo. This is a Buenos Aires number.'

'They're not letting foreign passports out,' I said.

'Damn,' Gerry said. There was a pause. 'So go to plan B. Nico can drive you out. Paraguay is easiest, the border's like a sieve.'

'Nico's no good, Gerry. He sold me out.'

'What happened?'

'I came back from the ferry terminal and my apartment had been ripped apart.'

There was a brief silence. 'Son of a bitch. They told me he was clean.'

'I don't have time to talk about it. How can I get out?'

'I'll manage it. I'm going to make some calls. Call me again tomorrow?'

I wanted something now, today, that I could take back with me to James's apartment. Some bit of a plan. I sighed. 'All right.'

'What's it like on the street?'

'Soldiers everywhere.'

'All right, then. Get back inside.'

I hung up and hurried back to the apartment, turning on the radio again. James arrived ten minutes after I did with a copy of El País. The newsagent had told him that a neighbor down the block, a Brazilian journalist who'd lived in Buenos Aires for twenty years, had been dragged out of his apartment at dawn by police and came limping home a day later, his face bruised and his hands shaking. The newspaper James brought was three days old, but he had only discovered it when he was already on his way home. Wanting to be occupied and inconspicuous, I read the paper even though it was completely useless. There was an article about an American minesweeper sinking in an accident off Puerto Rico. A hostile review of a James Bond film. A corn blight in some country where it was summer.

'There was no speech,' I said.

'No speech?'

'Onganía gave no speech,' I said. 'When they swore him in. They said on the radio just before you got back.' I was chewing my nails. James made instant coffee and brought me a mug.

'Everything looks normal outside, except for all the police,' James said. 'The banks are closed, but that's it. People are doing their grocery shopping. Kids are going into the school on Tucumán. I wonder how long it will last.'

On Thursday the newspaper was new and the radio was

reporting that the deposed president's brother had been arrested, taken away by the police while the two of them were sitting down to lunch at the brother's house somewhere on the fringes of the city. I hovered near the window through the morning and gleaned absolutely nothing at all from watching traffic go by on the street below. There was a feeling of being hemmed in invisibly, as if I were contained in a glass box. I forced James to accept money in exchange for the groceries he had bought in the market around the corner, and then insisted further on spending most of the short winter afternoon making a ragù, because idling in the living room with his paperbacks was beginning to make me insane. Just before curfew, I went out again to use the pay phone. I told James I was trying to get in touch with my mother.

Gerry sounded tense, his voice attenuated, as if he weren't speaking directly into the phone. 'Our contacts there are lying low,' he said.

'Of course they are,' I said. 'What's the plan?'

'If I can get the right person on the phone, we can get a special emergency visa for you. You'll get through the port, no problem. But.'

I stared at a cluster of patrolmen on the opposite corner. They had stopped a shabbily dressed young man and were making him empty his pockets.

'But you can't get the right person on the phone,' I supplied.

'Not yet. It's too chaotic, my dear. I'm trying.'

They were putting handcuffs on the young man. My stomach was cramping.

'You understand that I'm trying, don't you?' Gerry said.

'I do,' I said.

'Here's the thing. I need you to keep trying too. There's been an uptick in KGB activity all over Buenos Aires. They're on the move. You hear me? I know you're in a tough spot now, but this is no time to drop the mission. This is the opening they've been looking for. It could all come apart now, the whole theater.'

It was beginning to rain. I pulled the collar of my coat up. 'What do you want me to do? I dumped my equipment, Gerry.'

'Those boys you tracked – the ones in the warehouse –whatever they're planning, it's getting close. We intercepted a call from the Soviet embassy that went through a Brazilian exchange last night. The tone was very clear. They're activating their cells in the Southern Cone.'

'What should I do?'

'Destroy their capacity.'

'How?' A number of James Bond scenarios went through my mind. 'I'm a tech, Gerry. I don't do this kind of thing.'

'Think harder.'

'I could call it in to the police.'

'Bingo. Call me again when you can.'

'All right.'

I walked back slowly, thinking of Román in jail and trying not to think of it at the same time. He had been kind to me, in an unassuming way: pausing in a doorway when he saw I had fallen behind the group, pulling an extra chair from another table when I arrived last at the bar. He had a fluency with people that came from knowing he was welcome, that the students of the UC were always glad to see him coming. I felt sure that he felt safe, even now. That he had never felt unsafe, didn't know what it was. I felt cold. He took his bicycle, week after week, to that warehouse in La Boca. He packed a lunch, probably – I thought of the Coke I had seen on the worktable – and spent afternoons there, planning this thing. Gerry said he had bought

157

enough explosives in Paraguay to kill a dozen people.

Back in the apartment, the radio was taking a wildly optimistic tone, and James had kept the ragù from burning. The financial markets had reopened that morning. They were up, considerably. It was a glorious new dawn for the Argentine economy. An early winter twilight fell, with a perfunctory rustling and cawing of crows on the balcony. It was strange to remember that it was the last day of June. At around six o'clock the news came through that the mayor of Buenos Aires had been arrested. I found myself adding the same herbs over and over again to the bubbling pot, unable to remember what I had already done.

We played cards. James smoked incessantly. He found a bottle of wine, which we drank with the pasta and ragù.

'What does your father do?' he said.

'He's dead,' I said.

James squinted through his cigarette smoke at the cards in his hand in a way he probably thought was dashing. It was kind of dashing, actually.

'Can never quite square on you,' he said. 'Always one step ahead.'

'It's the truth,' I said. 'He died a long time ago. I was twelve.'

'I didn't mean you were lying. I'm not sure what I meant. I'm sorry.' He rubbed his forehead. 'It feels like we've been here together for weeks.'

It had been three days. 'Are you tired of me already?' I said, trying to be light.

'Who gets tired of a pretty girl?'

He insisted on the sofa that night, and I slept in the bed. In the middle of the night I got up to pee and paused for a moment in the living room, watching him sleep. He looked younger without his glasses.

In the morning he went out to visit his bank. After he left, I pulled on gloves and a hat and went quietly down the stairs. This would be my best opportunity to make the call to the police. I walked a few blocks, cutting carefully away from the busy street where James's bank was. Workmen waited at bus stops; children straggled to school. The scene was close to normal, but there was a hush over Buenos Aires. Voices carried with peculiar sharpness. I found a pay phone in front of a butcher shop and asked Information to connect me to the headquarters of the Buenos Aires police.

'I'd like to report a terrorist plot,' I said.

A mild male voice on the other end told me that this was serious, and that I should be sure that I was serious before saying it.

'I am serious,' I said. 'I can give you an address.'

'Please proceed, miss.'

I gave the address in La Boca. 'There's a crate full of explosives under a workbench against the north wall.'

'How did you obtain this information, miss?'

'I can't tell you that.'

'This is a serious matter. You will need to come into the station to speak with a detective.'

'I won't do that. If you don't want this information, I'll hang up right now.'

'No, miss, don't hang up. Describe the crate, please.'

I gave as much detail as I could about the crate, the room, and the building, and then I hung up. An old woman in a lavender raincoat came out of the butcher shop, holding a package wrapped in paper, which leaked blood. She stared at me. I moved away down the street.

In my secret heart, I admitted that I hoped Román and his friends weren't at the warehouse when it was raided. Some part of me couldn't believe that they did what they did in earnest. I thought they had to be mistaken somehow, misled. I hoped their supplies would be taken away and their plot ruined, and the episode would bring home to them how stupid they were being, and they would give up play-acting like revolutionaries.

I hurried back toward the apartment. At a corner, a group of soldiers were smoking and watching the street, bored looks on their faces, rifles strapped across their backs. I considered crossing to the other sidewalk, but decided it would only call more attention to me. They stopped me, not by raising a hand or speaking but by drifting into my path. Two in the front looked like they thought this was an excellent game. One put his hand out.

I looked inquiringly at his face. 'Papers?' I said. He smiled, but still refused to speak. There was a sick feeling in the back of my throat. I pulled my passport from my bag and gave it to him, and he thumbed it open, looked at it longer than he needed to, and handed it back. He took a very small step out of my way, enough so I would know I was free to go but not enough to keep me from having to brush against him as I passed.

Going up the stairs in James's apartment building, my heel caught in the hem of my dress and ripped it. In the living room, I hunted around in my bag until I found the clamshell sewing kit, relieved to have something to do.

When James came back from the bank he was agitated, his hair disordered, his coat wet from the rain. He lit a cigarette the moment he was inside the apartment.

'My account is frozen,' he said.

I stopped what I was doing and took a pin out of my mouth,

surprised.

'Foreign accounts are all frozen,' he said. 'Yours must be as well.'

I had no bank account, but I said nothing. I wondered if this might be good, actually. It would make him feel trapped, like I was. Tilt the balance so that I wasn't so aware at every moment of being at a disadvantage to him.

'You have cash, don't you?' he said.

We watched each other for a moment. During my time in Argentina I had lived on rubber-banded stacks of cash, counted out for me at the post office counter where they handled wire transfers from overseas.

'Yes,' I said, putting another tiny stitch in my dress.

'Well, all right,' he said. 'So we won't go hungry, anyway.' His shoulders came down a bit; he relaxed. I was touched. He didn't have a suspicious mind. He wasn't thinking about how to trick the money out of me. He assumed I would share it because we were stuck here together. And I would. Why wouldn't I? He was helping me. He came over to my chair and looked down at what I was doing.

'You're handy,' he said, and there was a pause, the length of a shallow breath, and he put his hand on my shoulder.

'You can't sew?' I said. I didn't turn my head.

'You have obviously never been to Texas,' he said. 'Of course I can't sew.'

My hair was pinned up. He brushed his fingers over the back of my neck. A smooth gesture, as if he were stroking the feathers of a bird and didn't want to startle it.

'The bank manager took me into a back room,' he said. 'I think he was enjoying it. This whole situation–' He fell quiet. 'It didn't seem real before. I thought it was kind of a technicality.

But now it's – I'm a little afraid.'

I leaned into his hand. He bent down and kissed me. I liked him, even if he did seem silly sometimes, a person who had always been well taken care of. He was generous, without thinking much about it. He assumed generosity in me that no one had seen or expected in a long time. I caught a handful of the front of his shirt.

I kept thinking we might go into the bedroom, but we didn't. It was a bit rushed, as if we might miss our chance if we paused or spoke to each other. Afterward we lay on the rug for a while, partly covered by his jacket, and I tried to think where I was in the month. Toward the end. I would be all right. He would feel better having me around, I thought, if this was part of it. I stroked the back of his head.

'Where'd you come from?' he said.

'Far, far away.'

'What a coincidence,' he said. 'Me too.'

JANUARY 1960. GREENWICH VILLAGE, NEW YORK CITY

After I spent the night at Sheila's, I walked around for weeks feeling as if there were spotlights on me, as if everyone could see what I was thinking and remembering, as if a vice squad might erupt out of nowhere at any moment. For a while I couldn't even walk past the Bracken, or any of the other gay bars that I knew of in the neighborhood. My preoccupation was so intense that I thought a raving bum on Broadway was shrieking 'Dyke!' at me when in fact it was 'Kike!' which I realized with intense relief. It was five months before I worked up the courage to flirt again, to meet another girl, and because it had hurt my feelings when Sheila didn't call me, I didn't give this one my number.

Most of my other friends pretended to be so worldly and louche that homosexuality hardly merited discussion, which sometimes struck me as an excuse to avoid discussing it. Even when a bar near the boarding house was raided, and the police marched out columns of women in cuffs while men jeered from across the street, my roommate never said a word.

JULY 1966. BUENOS AIRES, ARGENTINA

Three days later it was in the paper: BOMBING PLOT THWARTED. Several pounds of explosives found in a river-front warehouse. EVIDENCE OF COMMUNISTS IN THE VERY HEART OF ARGENTINA, said the headlines. The warehouse had been empty when they raided it. They must have staked it out first, I thought. Did Román see them, and stay away? I read and reread the articles, listened to all the bulletins on the radio. It was the first clear action, the first cause firmly fixed to an effect, of my career with the CIA. Maybe I had saved a life. Lives.

When I spoke to Gerry he had seen the story already in the international pages of the Times. He was pleased, but insistent. He needed more. 'You have to follow up,' he said. 'You have to see your friends.'

'Victoria?' I closed my eyes and took a deep breath. A headache instantaneously spread across my temples.

'Yes, her, him, whoever you can. There's too much to learn.'

'Fine. But this is the last thing, yes?' I said. 'I'll be out of here soon?'

'You'll be out of there soon.'

I told James I was going to argue with the visa office, and

went to Victoria's apartment. The security guard was still there in the lobby, but the building seemed somehow even quieter, more sepulchral, than before. I knocked on her door twice, softly. She pulled it open, a scarf over her hair.

'Anne!' she said. 'God, it's nice to see you!'

I was brought back to the party so forcefully that I could almost smell it, the *choripanes* and cigarettes in the apartment. 'It's been a while,' I said.

'It's been since Román's birthday. God, I drank too much. Did I make a fool of myself?'

I blinked twice and smiled blandly. 'What do you mean?'

'I hardly remember it, the whole night.' She waved me in, not looking at me. 'I haven't seen you since Onganía came in. I tried to call you the day it happened, and didn't get you. And then things have just been – I should have tried again. Are you all right?'

'I'm fine,' I said. 'Are you? I read about the arrests at the university.'

'I wasn't at the protest, I had an exam. Román, though, they knocked him down. But it could have been worse.' She went to the kitchen, filled a kettle. 'You want mate?'

'Sure. He's all right then?'

'He had a bruise, a scrape. He was fine. But he went to Rosario, to calm his mother.'

'Is he coming back?'

'Of course.' She smiled from the kitchen doorway. 'We don't run away.'

She seemed calm, or perhaps only detached. While she lingered in the kitchen, I stood at her living room window, wondering how much she knew. Whether she was protecting Román now, whether he was really in Rosario. 'There were so many police on the way over here,' I ventured. 'A dozen at the subway station.'

'I haven't been out,' she said from the kitchen. 'The police have been much worse since – you know the bomb they found in La Boca?'

'I read about it,' I said.

'It's a good excuse for them. They've been beating people in the street. Yesterday I saw it happen myself from the window. And when they stop girls to check papers, they grab you all over. You can't do anything.'

'But you said you haven't been out?'

'I hear things.'

'Don't your parents worry about you?' I said.

'They want me to come home.' She came out of the kitchen with the *mate* and the kettle, a plate of cookies balanced on her arm.

'Are you going to go?' As I said it, I realized that I wanted her to go, to be safe at her parents' big house outside the city. But this was absurd. She was dangerous herself. It was easier for me to think sensibly when I was alone. She poured a generous cascade of sugar down the side of the mound of tea leaves, which was the way I liked it, since the tea was so bitter. She doused it in hot water and passed it to me. The scalding rush gave some clarity to my thoughts.

'I can't go,' she said.

'Why not?'

She took the *mate* back from me and filled it for herself. An expression of fatigue passed briefly over her face. 'If I go home, they won't let me leave again. I'll never get out.'

'What do you mean?'

'I had to argue for a whole year to make them send me to the university. They wanted me to marry when I was twenty, to a neighbor of theirs. I'm twenty-seven. Did you know that? They think I'll never get married. My mother prays about it. But I have to finish my degree.'

The sun broke through the cloudy day, and now, through the doorway, I could see the disorder of the kitchen: the sink was filled with dishes, and a chicken carcass lay exposed on the counter. The air in the apartment was stale, I noticed now. She looked thin.

'How long has it been since you went out?' I said.

'Oh, a day or two.' She concentrated. 'Two days.'

'You're so afraid?'

She frowned. 'Afraid, no. I never feel afraid. But I'm cautious when I need to be.'

'I didn't mean to offend you.'

She looked at me carefully. Then she refilled the *mate* and passed it to me. 'You should remember sometimes that this is different for Argentines. I'm not on a visa, Anne. This is my country.'

She knew, I thought. She knew everything about Román and the warehouse, and she was afraid, no matter what she said. She was lying low. Her fingernails were bitten.

'I'm worried, that's all,' I said. 'You look tired.'

She waved her hand dismissively.

'I'm scared myself,' I added, trying to be conciliatory. 'I've been at the Canadian consulate twice since it happened. They say they can't do anything.' I stood up. 'Let me tidy up.'

'No, no. You can't do that.'

'You're not feeling well, I can see it.'

I went into the kitchen and ran water in the sink. I heard her switch on the radio in the living room, and then the drone of the news. The words comunistas, subversivos. When I looked in on her again, she was asleep on the sofa, one foot dangling over the edge.

I took a few minutes to go through the papers on her desk, but found only class notes and a stack of letters from a grandmother in Mendoza. There was nothing under her mattress; the boxes in her closet contained only shoes.

Back in the living room, I caught my breath, straightened my blouse. She was still asleep, her arm crossed over her stomach. I pulled a blanket over her and quietly let myself out.

Gerry said I must be careful. 'They're backed into a corner now,' he said. 'They may be unpredictable. You've gotten all you can. We need to get you out.'

But he had no way to get me out. Every time I called him, he said he was working on finding me a visa, that he had another man to try, that it would be soon, very soon, but not yet. The American delegation had gone dormant and he was now working through the back channels of the Argentine state, or what remained of it, trying to call in favors. In the midst of this, he learned that Nico had disappeared, together with his wife.

The story was simple. It had all come out in the first weeks after the coup. Nico was a Peronista. Juan Perón and his old allies in Argentina, who had never stopped working for his return from exile, had seen an opportunity in the much-predicted coup. They had hoped to make Onganía look like a CIA puppet, to turn the people against him. With Illia gone and Onganía weakened, they could bring Juan Perón triumphantly home from Spain and reinstall him in the Casa Rosada. To that end, it now seemed clear, Nico had given me up to the Buenos

Aires police on the day of the coup. Nico had worked for years for Aliadas, for the CIA, pretending. Coming to my apartment with that gun – giving it to me, I thought now, so the police could find it later. The smile, taking cigarettes from my pack. Sitting with me in his own kitchen. In mine.

'What about the man he had follow me?' I said. 'Who was he really working for?'

'We can't be sure, now. It's thrown everything into chaos.'

'Christ.'

'We can't be sure where Nico is, either,' Gerry said. 'If we're lucky, he's left the country. But if he's still in Buenos Aires, he could be dangerous.'

'He doesn't know where I am,' I said.

The ports, the airport, and the bus stations were still closed to foreign passports. Onganía was on the radio talking about Argentine sovereignty and freedom from foreign influence. People were having their papers inspected on the bus.

On the street and in cafés, people were beginning to use the word dictador. There were rumors that a couple of journalists had disappeared in Córdoba, and that a meeting of the carpenters' union in La Boca had been broken up by police. A satirical magazine called Tía Vicenta published a cartoon that depicted Onganía as a fat walrus with a bristling mustache, and the magazine was shut down for a month. I felt a little sick when I heard this news. It boded badly for everyone if the general was this sensitive, if his dignity was so fragile.

I told James about the walrus cartoon. He had already heard.

'No sense of humor,' I said.

'None whatsoever.'

'It's like having a child in charge,' I said. 'The pettiness of it.' I was chewing my nail. I thought of the building-sized images of

Stalin and Mao, which were laughable and yet were not laughed at. Onganía so proud of his mustache. There was guilt mixed into my fear. The Americans liked him so much.

'Did we do this?' I said to Gerry, the next time I spoke to him.

'What do you mean?'

'This. All this. You know what I mean.'

'We only create conditions,' Gerry said.

'What does that mean?'

'It means what I said. You sound irritable.'

'They're cracking down harder because of the bomb plot,' I said. 'I've heard the chief of police talking about it on the radio. An excuse to tighten the curfew.'

'Well, that's standard operating procedure. I'm not surprised.'

I rubbed my chin. I had been grinding my teeth lately, and it was hurting my jaw.

'Maybe I should just try again with cash,' I said, meaning: make another run at the ferry terminal and hope for better luck this time.

'I can't recommend that. The whole country is in a very paranoid frame of mind right now.'

To soothe myself I went to department stores. As a child I had been comforted by the gold-trimmed counters at Bloomingdale's on Christmas trips with my mother; she was warm and surprising at those times, because she loved to spend money. She made a good living and had grown up with very little, and she bought me things that awed me, gloves and handbags stitched elaborately with seed pearls and silk thread, tiny cut-crystal bottles of perfume, winter coats trimmed with leather. Things I never asked for and didn't know how to handle or repair. When she gave me these things she would turn them over and inside out so I could see their construction. It was important to her that I understand how to spot cheap leather and bad shoes. I didn't understand then what she thought she was protecting me from. I understood better when I was grown up and on my own and had no money. It was love, when she towed me around the Junior Miss section and had arduous conversations with salesgirls. That was her at her best.

So I went to the Retiro neighborhood and spent afternoons in Harrods. It had lovely tiled floors. I took armfuls of dresses into the dressing rooms, which were lined with benches upholstered in plum velvet, and spent thirty or forty minutes at a time trying on silk crepe. I spoke as little as possible; I waved away the salesgirls, not wanting to display my foreign accent if I could avoid it. I read books in the Harrods tea shop and eavesdropped as the waitresses repeated rumors that the English had anchored a destroyer off the Falkland Islands. For a week or two that winter I heard that rumor everywhere on my short trips outside the apartment, in grocery stores and at newspaper kiosks. These stories of English perfidy in the islands always came up when the president of Argentina was unpopular, and they worked their magic, every time. There were fewer complaints about Onganía for a while. On a Tuesday I arrived at Harrods and found that someone had thrown a brick through one of the display windows, inside of which a mannequin's fur coat sparkled with crushed glass. Fuera de Argentina ingleses de mierda was painted on the wall. Harrods was of course a British enterprise. I stopped going there.

There were protests against Onganía in Córdoba, and during a melee with the police on one of the broad avenues, a student was shot. He hung on for five days in the hospital and then he died, and graffiti appeared on walls around the Universidad Central, his name and the dates of his birth and death. The messages were always painted over quickly but they kept reappearing. Bars where students liked to go were nearly empty. Plainclothes police lounged conspicuously in the windows.

APRIL 1960. MIDTOWN, NEW YORK CITY

After Con Edison, I got a job as the night girl at WVBI, the radio station. The nocturnal life appealed to me. The night shift, which began at eight o'clock in the evening, paid more than the day.

We worked on Forty-Sixth Street, across from a theater that cycled through cha-cha revues and a fur emporium where you could pay to have your minks stored in a refrigerated box. The night girl at WVBI was expected to sweep the floors, empty the ashtrays, brew coffee, and handle the switchboard for callers who wanted to dedicate songs.

We had an elderly engineer named Kirkland who began drinking at midnight and started missing his cues at two, and Hal, the station manager, handled it by making Kirkland teach me his trade so I could step in when he began to fade. Kirkland was offended by it at first, but he could see the use of it. He was about seventy years old, with a courtly manner that was not undone by the smell of bourbon in the air.

I liked the work. Things went awry and I learned to fix them. Kirkland taught me the thousand and one ways that a transmission can fail to be transmitted, and then fail to be received, and I enjoyed the range of these problems, from a squirrel nest in a transformer box to encrypted interference from navy destroyers off the coast. The air was full of radio signals.

My roommate moved out to live with her boyfriend in Hell's Kitchen, which meant that I had to find a new place, and that was a problem. My salary from the station was barely enough to keep me in deli sandwiches and replace my stockings when they ran. Landlords in decent buildings didn't want to rent to a single girl anyway. The first of the month came and I found myself in a dirtier boarding house, a place on Columbus Avenue where I shared a room with a nurse who kept bottles of gin hidden under her bed and sang to herself when she couldn't sleep. Before my shifts, while I tried to make coffee on a hot plate, I could hear the mice busy in the wall. Soon I was spending all my days off trying to find another place, a real apartment. I looked at a dozen cold-water flats in Hell's Kitchen, but no one would let me sign a lease, and every time I managed to save up the two months' rent that I would need upfront, some disaster took it away – a filling that had to be replaced, a week at home with the flu and no sick time to cover it.

As a child I had a book, clothbound, with intricate illustrations, that told the story of a squirrel, rabbit, and chipmunk who lived in a house together in the woods. The crumbling flyleaf was dated 1918. It had belonged to my father. In each chapter, the animals met and bested another challenge. The chapters matched the seasons of the year. In the winter chapter, their stores of nuts and seeds were swept away in a late flood, and they were left hungry. The rabbit, a cheerful character in the summer and autumn chapters, grew thin and sad in the illustrations. The animals did less and less, spoke less and less.

One moonlit night, the rabbit was awakened by scratching at the door. He looked out the window. A wolf was there.

The rabbit was changed by having seen the wolf. Spring came, and there were fresh shoots and grubs and eggs to eat, and the animals got fat again. But the rabbit's fur had turned gray.

It was during the week I spent in bed with the flu, wracked with fever and then aching with boredom, that I saw my wolf.

When I recovered, I went back to work. I used an X-Acto knife and the Ditto machine in the secretary's office to mock up a letter from the First Bank of Chevy Chase claiming I had fifty thousand dollars in trust. Then I went out to Brooklyn to look for apartments. Within a few weeks, a landlord accepted the fake trust letter, and I moved into a run-down apartment with tall windows on Eastern Parkway in Brooklyn.

Kirkland was expected to make monthly journeys to the station's transmitter in Queens to run maintenance checks. It was in Rockaway, out near the beach. He hated doing it; it was a long trip in the dead of night. I volunteered to go with him. By September I was making the trip by myself, finishing up at six in the morning.

If I had some fire left in me after running the checks I would go and sit on the boardwalk, pulling my skirt around my knees, drinking a paper cup of Lipton tea from a deli and watching the sun rise over the Atlantic. Then back to Brooklyn, nearly two hours, a knish eaten as I climbed the stairs to my apartment, a morning and an afternoon in bed. In my apartment on Eastern Parkway, the floors creaked and the radiators whistled when the heat came on at night. A brightly lit, steam-filled shop on the ground floor of the building sold the knishes that I liked, alongside trays of jam-filled cookies. Orthodox women in navy coats walked up and down the parkway with flocks of red-haired children. On Tuesdays – I never worked on Tuesdays – I would rise in the afternoon and walk down to the Central Library on Grand Army Plaza, check out a few mystery novels, and sit on the steps eating a chocolate doughnut and gazing up at the arch that honored the Union Army. At the top of it a woman stood in a chariot with horses rampant, attended by angels, a bronze banner unfurling over her head.

JULY 1966. BUENOS AIRES, ARGENTINA

I kept busy as well as I could while I waited for Gerry's plans to come through, cooking and cleaning, trying to fit into the domestic routines of a man used to doing for himself. I did the grocery shopping, glad to get out of the house.

One dark afternoon late in July, I went to the vegetable stalls to buy turnips and potatoes. My walk back to the apartment took me past one of the grand old public libraries in the Centro. A few yellow leaves still clung to a locust tree in front, slowing the drift of rain over a group of huddled students. With a start, I recognized Román among them, smoking a thin black cigarette. He looked whole and well, and I was relieved, and then felt a confused flush. I thought about speaking to him, but decided to delay contact, to watch him for a few minutes if I could. I crossed to the other side of the street and ducked inside a bakery.

I watched the students through the window, hidden by a rack of cooling challah. So Román was out of hiding. The students around him looked tense, but Román was the same as ever, smiling slightly, standing apart, as if a spotlight were on him. At the beginning of the academic year, when the afternoons were still long and hot, groups of students had stood in front of the facultad just like this, smoking and talking as they were doing now, and I had hovered nearby with Victoria's shy friend Elena while she tried to calculate a way into the circle. It had been only four months since then, but it felt much longer. I was sweating. Behind me, the baker cleared her throat and called out, 'We've got madeleines. Hot ones, out of the oven right now.'

'Oh, very nice,' I said. I waved my net bag. 'Madeleines, yes. A dozen.'

She nodded approvingly and began to fill a box. Román had ventured a few steps away from the group to talk to a pretty girl with long black hair. I wondered what Victoria would think of that. What did it mean that he had come back? He must have something in mind. It wasn't safe here for someone like him.

A smallish turnip worked its way silently through a frayed part of my bag and fell to the floor, and I bent quickly to pick it up.

The bell rang over the door, and there was Román, dropping the end of his cigarette behind him on the sidewalk and running his hands through wet hair.

'Anne!' he said to me, smiling, surprised.

'Román!' We kissed hello.

'We were worried about you,' he said. 'It's been hard for foreigners.'

'I've been worried about you too,' I said.

'They keep arresting people at the protests. The student union has been marching after evening classes. I got knocked around.' He brushed back his hair to show a dark scab at his hairline, just above his left ear.

'A baton?' I said, wincing.

'A fist.' He laughed. 'He split his knuckles open. Victoria says

I have a hard head.' He glanced back out at the street. 'It'll get worse, I think. Victoria and I won't stay long.'

'Where will you go?' I said.

'Ushuaia,' he said. He paused, as if he were trying to remember something, and then he turned to me again and said briskly, 'I have an uncle there.'

'That's far,' I said. It sounded like a nice idea, really.

'Very far,' he said. 'Very quiet. What will you do?'

'I'm waiting for a visa.'

'I hope you get one. Your family must be worried.'

He squeezed my arm; he was affectionate like this with all his friends. He went to the counter to order biscuits, and I waved goodbye and went back out to the street. I walked casually in the wrong direction for several blocks, in case he had seen which way I was going, and then circled idly for a while so I could think.

Ushuaia was a clutter of utilitarian buildings in the lap of a mountain at the tip of Tierra del Fuego. People called it 'the end of the earth,' a small city facing the Southern Ocean and Antarctica. Victoria and Román would have to cross hundreds of miles of cold desert to reach it. It was the kind of place where you went when you were afraid. It was so remote that it seemed like a myth.

That afternoon, when I called Gerry's service, he didn't call back at all. I stood for twenty minutes next to the phone box and smoked three cigarettes. Perhaps Gerry could do nothing. Perhaps he had known since the coup happened that he could do nothing. Perhaps all the people he was connected to in Buenos Aires were poisoned by contact with Nico.

I thought of Ushuaia again. A new plan was beginning to form. But first I had to be sure that Román was telling me the truth.

James and I shared the bed now. I woke early – I had never been a good sleeper – and lay beside him until he woke up too. I liked it best when he faced away from me and I could rest against his back, as if he were a low wall or a rise in the earth, and watch the sky lighten through the uncovered window; at those times he reminded me of a girl I used to know. She and I had played house for a while once, and we had lain like this; but I had too many secrets to keep by the time I met her, and I ended it. She always pushed. There was a soft down on the nape of her neck.

I modified a small transistor radio from a department store and sat in a park a block away from Victoria's building, listening to the bug from her apartment. When I felt that I had been there too long, I moved to a café down the street, and then to a back corner of a Christian Science Reading Room two doors down from her, where I could listen on headphones while I pretended to study a macroeconomics textbook. I was there when I heard the phone ring, and then Victoria's voice saying anxiously, 'When will the plane be ready?'

Román visited; I heard them discussing cold weather, the friend who would fly the plane, the grandfather who owned it. A little ranch plane, they said. There was excitement in their voices.

They talked about the ocean, about penguins.

OCTOBER 1962. CROWN HEIGHTS, BROOKLYN, NEW YORK

On the morning of October 23 the telephone in my apartment woke me, clattering furiously on the wall in the kitchen. I had been deeply asleep, having arrived home at 6:00 AM, and my heart was hammering when I fumbled it off the wall. Everyone knew not to call me until well into the afternoon.

'Hello?' came the faint Southern voice.

'Ma?'

'Vera, thank God. Have you been reading the news?'

There had been no exchange between us since her last letter to me at the Barrington School. For a second I was sure that someone had died: My grandmother. Joanne. I could hear the newsroom in the background. 'What's wrong, Ma? What happened?'

'Kennedy is blockading Cuba. They're out there in destroyers. He was on television last night. We had to tear up the next issue of the magazine and start over.'

My mind cleared. The Soviet missiles in Cuba. I put my hand over my heart. 'Jesus, Ma, I thought somebody must be dead.'

'You should pay attention to the news,' she said. 'This could be war.'

'It won't be war,' I said, but I was thinking about how they had explained it to us when we were kids in school: a flash of light. They had said it that way so we wouldn't think about the heat, I thought, or the noise, but it had not reassured me, the idea of a light at the end of the world. 'How did you get this number, Ma?'

She laughed her big laugh. 'I put a reporter on it.'

'This is what you call about?' I said. 'After all this time?'

'I was worried about you.'

'Just now, you were? Well, I'm fine.'

'I don't want to be angry with you anymore, Vera. Not with all this going on. I want to be reconciled.'

I took the phone away from my ear so that I could look at it. I turned in a circle. Then I spoke into it again. 'I have no idea what you think I could do,' I said, 'to make you not be angry with me anymore.'

'An apology,' she said. 'Be a human being.'

'Good luck with the new issue.' I pressed the phone back into the cradle.

Five days after my mother called me, Khrushchev started taking apart the missiles and the tabloids stopped shrieking about annihilation. But I still felt that flinch in the air.

SEPTEMBER 1966. BUENOS AIRES, ARGENTINA

New morality laws had been passed, and they were printed in the papers every Sunday, in case anyone might forget them. Onganía's prudishness seemed sincere, a rare thing for the military men. He forbade kissing in public, dim lighting in bars, miniskirts. In each of these new statutes, I saw the shadow of the vice-squad raids back home, although homosexuality was mentioned nowhere. I caught myself checking mirrors before I left the apartment, putting on more lipstick, as if carefully reviewing a disguise.

I saw a group of young women getting official warnings for their skirts one unseasonably warm evening. They all had black hair teased up into beautiful bouffants and eyes lined thickly with kohl, like Elizabeth Taylor in Cleopatra, and they stood with their arms crossed while a very young and pink-faced cadet lectured them. They made me think of my days at eighteen, the first summer after the Barrington School, walking back to the boarding house arm-in-arm with a friend who later stole ten dollars from my purse and bought me lunch with half of it. There were so many young men and women around me then whom I wouldn't leave alone with my wallet. And yet I took those betrayals so lightly. How inconsequential they seemed compared to the force and energy of our interest in each other, because we had read some of the same books and grown tired of the same schools and we had all run away from our parents. What was ten dollars when you had the same blood in your veins? I wished for the girls in miniskirts to have the same chances in their lives to injure each other and be injured.

There was a club on the corner of James's street where we went a few times to dance when we were beginning to go stir-crazy in the apartment. They had a house band: a girl singer in blue sequins and a blonde wig that glittered like tinsel, a quartet of young men behind her in black jackets. Whenever one of the boys took the microphone, they would sing covers of the Stones.

The clientele was young, many of them barely out of high school. In the corners, girls in outrageous makeup gathered, too shy to talk to boys. The boys smoked constantly, their backs to the room. James and I would sit by the door, drinking pale beer in tall glasses. Many of the younger patrons of the bar ordered nothing but Coca-Cola all night, and I was touched by it. The caffeine and sugar gave them energy to dance, and they had no money for anything stronger. If the place got too loud, the owner – a small, fat man with sideburns razored to points – would become apoplectic, waving his short arms and demanding quiet from a jostling throng that couldn't hear him.

The law said that the lights in bars had to be bright enough to read the labels on the bottles. One Friday night in the club, as James and I were dancing to a cover of a Zombies song, the lights at the back of the house switched on. There was an immediate impression of dust and concrete in the yellow light; we were in a basement, which we easily forgot when it was dark. The band stopped playing. The girl in the blonde wig bit her lip and muttered 'Hijo de–' into the microphone, then set it down on top of the amplifier and stared down at her feet. Police filed in through the narrow street door.

'Out, out, out,' they called, shining flashlights around the room. Two officers led a group of boys and girls outside. The girls were stone-faced, the boys sullen. There was a scuffle near the bar. James put his arm around me and we moved through the uncertain crowd, trying not to draw too much attention to ourselves.

We had to push through the group of police to get out, which made my heart pound, but they parted before us. Their attention was occupied by the fight at the bar, which was drawing in more young men. We slipped out onto the quiet street, and I stopped to take a deep breath. The night air was humid and cool, smelling of the river. Halfway up the block, waiting and smoking a cigarette, was the man in the gray raincoat.

We saw each other. James didn't notice. I stared at the man and then turned quickly away. James was saying that he hoped the kids were okay. He was soft-hearted. I rubbed my face, pulled my jacket on. My head hurt and I was afraid. It was over. I was out of time.

NOVEMBER 1962. CROWN HEIGHTS, BROOKLYN, NEW YORK

One afternoon not long after I spoke to my mother, I was trying to handle a short circuit in an electrical closet at the station during a rare day shift when a man with a pomaded wave in his hair appeared at my elbow and introduced himself. He was a consultant, he said.

'Nice to meet you,' I said.

'What are they paying you?' he said cheerfully. 'I bet it's not enough.'

I took a closer look at him.

'I might have some work for you,' he said. 'An electronics outfit in Jersey. They're looking for people. Something on the side.' He glanced up and down the hallway as if anxious that we not be seen, and I couldn't be sure if this was a joke or not. He handed me a card. 'I'm not poaching you. It would be extra.'

'Oh. Well, thank you.' I examined the card. Consulting. An address on the east side and a phone number.

The man shook my hand and irradiated me with his smile. 'Really, give me a call,' he said.

The fact was, I didn't make enough money, and my landlord was threatening to terminate my lease if I bounced another check.

It had been keeping me from my sleep. I called the number on the consultant's card and a secretary gave me the address of a shop in Jersey City.

I appeared dutifully at a storefront on Warren Street on a foggy Tuesday morning and rang the bell. The blinds were closed and the place looked deserted. At last an old man opened the door and ushered me through a front office that looked abandoned and into a large back room. It was a place that could have been used comfortably for car repair, with raw brick walls, a poured concrete floor, and high cobwebbed windows facing a narrow alley and the back of a church. Four workbenches were piled with wiring, sheets of copper, switches, and Mylar.

'What do I do?' I said to the old man.

'You make circuit boards,' he said.

Now I spotted the billiard-table green of a stack of circuit boards on the workbench.

'Those are all dead,' he said. 'Fix the ones you can. Then make copies of the ones that are working.'

So I worked in the shop every Tuesday for two months, with a stack of circuit boards growing at my elbow. I was paid well for this work, suspiciously well, and in cash. By January, when the consultant finally appeared at the shop without warning one afternoon, I had an idea of where this was going.

'You're doing well here,' he said jovially.

My elbows and back were sore. I had cuts on my fingers, dabbed up with Mercurochrome. 'Is my audition over?' I said.

He sat down on the other side of my bench. His expression shifted. The fluorescent smile changed, became slightly more ordinary. He regarded me across the bench, and for the first time I saw the intelligence in his eyes, like a flicker of static electricity.

'I mean,' I went on, faltering now but trying to brazen it out, 'you're one of those CIA men, aren't you? Or State Department?'

A jazz DJ at the station had told me months ago that the men in suits who sometimes visited the business office were propagandists from the CIA, a claim I had dismissed until I observed them for a while myself and noticed the news stories we ran after they visited. I had been thinking about this moment for weeks, wondering if it would come, telling myself periodically that I was crazy. It was possible that the job might simply be what it claimed to be. But as time went on I had become more confident that I was being recruited, and it was making me edgy, distracting me on the long rides home after work in the dawn hours, setting me off on reveries during the slow nights at the station. What would it mean if it were true? A secret life, I thought. Independence. More money than I needed. I hoped for all that. I couldn't quite bring into focus what I would lose. It would be dangerous. But I was twenty-two years old and couldn't take any danger to my person seriously.

'The intelligence services have roles for women,' he said. 'You understand electronics. You speak Spanish and French.'

'How do you know that?'

He kept smiling calmly at me, as if I had asked a rhetorical question.

'You've been looking at my school records?' I said.

'My boss was concerned about the Maryland Youth Center,' he said. 'But I pushed for you.'

'Where did you get my records?'

'The next theater of war is Latin America,' he said.

He said this the way a person might say, 'On Fridays the cafeteria serves fish.' A car in the street outside was failing to start. It coughed and whined. Dust motes floated in the air above his head.

'Cuba?' I said.

'Central America, South America, the Caribbean.'

'What are we talking about?' I said.

'Surveillance.'

I cleared my throat. 'Are you offering me a job?'

'Yes, a job,' he said, smiling more brightly. 'That's a good way to think of it.'

I was confused. 'How else could I think of it?'

'A life,' he said.

We studied each other. I said, 'People get killed doing this kind of work.'

'Yes,' he said. 'The CIA would do everything possible to protect you. You see what's happening in the Eastern Bloc. What they did to the students in Hungary. Cuba is just the beginning. The jails in Havana are full of political prisoners. The Soviets are behind them with ballistic missiles. We're at war.'

I said nothing. I had seen photos of the uprising in Hungary, students who were later shot. I was thinking of how helpless I had felt on the phone with my mother when she called about the missiles.

'What's keeping you here?' he said finally.

SEPTEMBER 1966. BUENOS AIRES, ARGENTINA

The day after I saw the man in the gray raincoat outside of the nightclub, I embarked on my plan and went to see Victoria in the evening. I hadn't slept; I'd lain awake all night imagining the police breaking down the door of the apartment. My appetite was gone, and when I passed a mirror in the lobby of Victoria's building I was surprised by my own white face.

Victoria seemed fresh and at ease. She was happy to see me. She sat on her cherry-red love seat, smoking, her hair so newly pressed that I could still see the creases from the hot rollers. A Brazilian rock band played on the radio. School papers were strewn across the floor.

'Román told me you were leaving town,' I said.

'Tomorrow. We have a friend who's a pilot,' she said. 'We chartered a ranch plane from an airstrip out in the country. It's safer that way, if we don't have to go through Ezeiza Airport. They might be watching us.'

She wouldn't look at me, and then she wouldn't look away, smiling like a moll trying to distract a cop. 'It's not safe here, you know that,' she said. 'Not for people like us.'

'Like – us?' I said.

'Me and Román,' she said.

I remembered the party again, the scuffle by the bathroom door. She always seemed to be both insinuating and withholding, the two held in tension in a way that baffled and angered me and made me feel stupid. She was looking at me now as if she were also remembering the party, and at the same time as if I were a stranger who had wandered too close to her on a subway platform.

'It's not safe for me either,' I said.

She scoffed. 'You're fine. You're Canadian.'

'I can't get a visa. A group of French students were arrested last week for subversion, did you see that in the paper? It's not safe to be foreign here now.'

She looked at a stack of paperbacks on the floor in front of her. Several crumbling editions of Erich Fromm. 'It's a complicated time.'

'I have to leave Buenos Aires,' I said. 'I want to come with you to Ushuaia.'

She looked shocked. She laughed and shook her head. 'Absolutely not. Absolutely not, it's not possible.'

I was making no effort to hide my desperation, because I thought it would move her, but she didn't care. From Ushuaia I could find a tanker that would take me through the Strait of Magellan and around to the Chilean side of the Andes. It was the only way I could get out of Argentina without showing papers.

'You have to let me,' I said.

'This is ridiculous. God, everything...' She waved her hand at the living room. 'I hardly know you. You don't know what you're asking.'

'Why have you flirted with me all this time?' I said. I didn't mean to say it, it burst out, and then I was ashamed. I sat down abruptly in a chair. 'You were playing some stupid game. Do you think I'm a child?' My face was burning. 'Try your tricks on someone else.'

She sat up straight in surprise, her cigarette drifting close to her Lustre-Creme-scented hair, all innocence. I doubted myself again, it was so persuasive.

'I've only tried to be your friend,' she said.

'Then be my friend, carajo,' I said. 'Let me on that fucking plane. Or I'll tell Román you made a pass at me.'

She turned white. Her gaze was flat and miserable.

'You don't understand,' she said, and her eyes welled up with tears. She got up and came over to me, crouched on the floor beside my chair, and gripped both my elbows. Her touch felt hot and sticky, as if it might leave a residue on my skin. I pulled away.

'That would be a mistake,' she said. 'That would be for nothing. I can't let you come with us. Please don't tell Román. But I can't let you come. I'm sorry if it's dangerous for you here, I am, I really am. I want you to be safe. But this thing you're asking for, I can't do.' She stood up. 'Román is coming. He'll be here in a few minutes. You have to go. I'm so sorry, so sorry. Please don't be angry.' She hunched over me, stroking my hair. I ducked away. 'Please, please,' she said. 'You have to go. There's no choice.'

Out on the street I had to collect myself, breathing deeply and pretending to search for something in my purse. It was a cold night despite the distant approach of spring. A mist in the air was becoming rain. I had no choice either. I would have to get on the plane. It would mean a scene; it would mean, perhaps, digging Nico's pistol up out of its hiding place. I stood in a bus shelter, my hands and feet slowly going numb. The bus didn't come. I walked back to the apartment on Calle Riobamba.

In the hall outside the door I stopped and listened to the warm crackle of Billie Holiday. James had a lot of jazz records I didn't like much, jostling abstractions that I suspected him of not liking very much himself. He would put them on and sit frowning on the sofa with a glass of whiskey, as if he were receiving bad news. But the Billie Holiday records I liked, and Sarah Vaughan, and the libidinous Etta James, which I sometimes put on myself when he was out. I liked the way she scratched and pushed. James was usually in a good mood if those records were playing. And I could smell seared beef. He would be cooking and drinking wine. He had a bachelor's self-sufficiency.

I pulled a mirrored compact out of my purse and stood under the hall light. My eyes were red, my skin pale from fear in a way that made me look yellow; I brushed on rouge and combed and re-pinned my hair. You are tired but feeling well. You have been shopping on Rivadavia for a new raincoat all afternoon but you couldn't find anything you liked.

He had left the door unlocked for me. I stepped inside, hung up my coat and hat, strode into the kitchen.

'Steaks?' I said.

'They were cheap today,' he said.

I went into the living room and sat down. I tried to pet the cat but she darted away. I sat for a moment with my hands on my knees and looked out through the uncurtained windows. We were so visible in here. James said he wasn't embarrassed by anything, and anyway he didn't know how or where to buy curtains, how to cut them to measure, how to stitch the hems. So interesting that a person could live that way. That both his needs and his skills could be so different from mine. I watched him through the doorway of the kitchen. He was humming to himself.

The thing that was wrong with me was that the intimacy and safety of this apartment felt real to me even though it was false. I was duping and manipulating him, and still somehow I felt I deserved his tokens of affection, his small gestures of protection and care, this steak he was cooking now to my specifications, more well-done than he liked his own. I was so easily taken in by my own illusion, so quick to accept the generosity I tricked out of others. If he found out who I really was and how I had lied he would be shocked and betrayed and he would be right. And yet I would be startled and put out, if it came to that. Because it felt all right to me, all of this. It felt nice.

From the street outside I must look very small, I thought. The ceilings were high. There was so much wall behind me.

He was in a talkative mood. He had gotten another letter from home. He could do a funny impersonation of his father, who had a Mexican accent broadened and slowed by his decades in Texas, and he quoted bits of the letter in this accent. His father wanted him to come home, always. James was burdened by this. He hated leather. He hated Houston. He had never had an ambition for himself that hadn't been chosen by someone else. He wanted to know who he might be if he were left alone.

'Does your mother get at you to come home?' he said.

'No,' I said. I laughed. 'No, she doesn't.'

'Do you hear from her?'

'Not often.'

He was looking at me curiously, but I didn't look back. 'She doesn't approve of you?' he said.

'No.' My mother with her long beaked nose and delicate hair.

Tall and broad across the shoulders, impressive in her best suits in a way that unnerved people, that unnerved me, a woman like a tree, resisting any effort to scale her down, even in my imagination.

'Every girl I've ever been with thought her mother was a monster.'

I didn't like it when he acted knowing like that. I was probably not meant to like it. 'My mother had me put in jail when I was seventeen.'

Billie Holiday filled up the short silence that ensued. I thought my anger might be spent with that, but no, there was some left. 'Not everyone has an empire to go home to,' I said, and then it was all gone and I deflated in my chair.

He was generous. He let it go by. 'Why did she do it?' he said finally.

'She beat the hell out of me and I ran away in her car. She had me arrested for stealing it.'

'You look sad.'

'I'm just tired,' I said.

'A long day?'

'I was looking for a new raincoat on Rivadavia,' I murmured, 'but I didn't find anything I liked.'

FEBRUARY 1963–JANUARY 1966. CARTAGENA, COLOMBIA / ACAPULCO, MEXICO / TEGUCIGALPA, HONDURAS / MARACAY, VENEZUELA

My first assignment was a trade convention in Colombia in February 1963, a small thing, a long weekend in the field, using a few vacation days I had saved up at the station. For this long weekend, I was paid a thousand dollars in cash. My yearly salary at the station at that time came to two thousand dollars.

I was put up in the conventioneers' hotel in Cartagena and had to train myself not to blush and stare at the floor whenever I found myself in an elevator with a man wearing a conference badge. I was booked into a room between the Finnish delegation and the French delegation, and I spent four days crouched on the floor eating sticky grapes and listening to conversations about nightclubs and cab fares in French while my recording equipment hissed unattended over the Finns on the other side of the room. The consultant had done the booking; he referred to himself now as my handler. I had to transcribe the French conversations, and they were of a towering dullness that began to approach comedy as the nights in the hotel room wore on. I have not called my wife. The international rates are a crime. There is an insect in the bathtub. An insect in the bathtub? Yes, I saw it. This city is filthy. But have you seen the churches on the square, very lovely. Yes, very lovely, but there are insects in the bathtub and we are served instant coffee.

The rooms were easy to set up, in that hotel. My handler had spent a long time training me, giving me exercises. It was a pretty small-bore operation, overall, and if any real intel came out of it, I never heard. But I was wild with excitement anyway when I returned to New York. I felt like a girl in a movie. I felt like my life had begun.

I was in Mexico when President Kennedy was shot. I was staying in a tourist hotel by the water in Acapulco, and I came back from the beach to find the lobby filled with stunned and weeping Americans, a TV hastily set up on a dinner cart in the corner. My handler ended the assignment two days early, and I sat in the departures lounge at the airport with a handkerchief pressed to my face, leaking tears.

The level I operated on was small. My assignments were orderly trips with little risk to me, conferences where I spent a few days making recordings and then returned to New York, and when I got back home I could resume my life again as if I had never been away. Everything was small until Buenos Aires.

My handler pitched it to me in January 1966, in a diner where he liked to meet on East Fifty-Second Street. The Argentine president was weak, there could be a coup anytime, and KGB activity had picked up in Buenos Aires. I would have to do infiltration work as well as surveillance. I would be gone indefinitely, months or a year, and I would have to quit my job. For this they would pay me thirty-five thousand dollars.

'This is what you've been waiting for, isn't it?' Gerry said. He slid a new passport across the table, a Canadian one this time. 'Something big.'

I stared at the passport. He put his hand on mine. 'Think about it,' he said. 'But not too long.'

I was distracted that night at work, and I hardly slept after my shift was over. It had been a bitterly cold January, and I lay listening to the radiator clang until midmorning. Finally admitting to myself that I wouldn't sleep, I pulled on a sweater and heavy coat and went for a walk down the icy parkway. My feet quickly went numb. It had begun to snow, a whispering light snow that I knew would stick. I turned into Prospect Park. The snowy trees formed a white lace against a soft gray sky. The great lawn was empty except for a distant figure with a dog.

I imagined my life if this work wasn't in it anymore. The excitement and sense of purpose that I had felt coming back from those long weekends, gone. Scraping by forever on thirty-eight dollars a week.

Three days later I stood in the departures line at LaGuardia, holding a one-way ticket with AEROPUERTO EZEIZA printed across it in heavy black type and clutching the new passport, which gave my name as Anne Patterson.

SEPTEMBER 1966. BUENOS AIRES, ARGENTINA

I sat up late listening to the radio, thinking I wasn't going to be able to sleep anyway. After James went to sleep I packed my few things into the brown suitcase and left it by the door, hidden under my overcoat. I smoked three of the cigarettes he always kept in a silver box by the window, listening to an orchestra play. A woman's voice trilled up ahead of the band from time to time. I had seen couples dancing the tango in the bars in San Telmo, and was struck by the way they handled each other, as if they were made of bone china. They didn't look at each other much. They kept their eyes down, looking at their hands or the floor, as if lost in separate thoughts. They sometimes leaned on each other, and sometimes pulled apart, examining each other's faces briefly and then pressing close again.

At two o'clock in the morning I went into the bedroom and climbed in beside James. He stirred but didn't wake.

At four I woke up again, pulled on my crumpled skirt and blouse, and washed my face in the cramped bathroom. At the front door I took the pistol out of the packed suitcase and stood looking at it. It was so heavy in my hand, even though it was unloaded. The radio was still playing, very low; I turned it off. The box of bullets was in the suitcase.

I put six bullets in the gun. As I finished I glanced up and saw my reflection in the window, a girl dressed like a legal secretary holding a gun without authority. I straightened my blouse with my free hand. I tried to clear the anxiety out of my face. It didn't help. The girl in the window raised the gun and aimed: she looked ridiculous. I clicked the chamber open and emptied the gun, let the bullets rattle back into the box, and put the pistol in my purse.

Outside the streets were hushed, the sky still dark. I walked out to the avenue and hailed a cab, and then sat rigidly alert in the back as the driver murmured and chattered. Dawn was breaking; the sky over Puerto Madero was turning gray, and then the pink of the inside of a shell. Soon we had left the density of the city and turned onto a straight two-lane road that rolled on for miles past rows of leafless young tipa trees, their branches sinuous and black against the sky. Flocks of black birds were beginning to stir. After all this time I was unprepared for the quiet outside of the city, which I could feel even through the grumbling of the car. My stomach had become dense and hard. I hadn't eaten in hours but couldn't imagine making any attempt at breakfast, even when the driver stopped with apologies at a gas station to fill the tank and asked gallantly if I wanted a hot biscuit or empanada from the whitewashed cantina at the edge of the lot.

The airport that Victoria had mentioned was small and alone in a vast open space. Lights twinkled from a low sheet-metal building at the far end of a long dirt runway; in the distance, poplar windbreaks divided fields of tall grass, and black cows huddled beside the brush of a stream. On a pitted tarmac half a dozen small planes waited, painted cheerfully with stripes.

I couldn't go into the building because that was where

Victoria and Román and their friends would be, and I couldn't let them see me until the last moment. I paid the driver and pulled my suitcase out of the trunk, and he reversed and turned slowly and bumped over the holes in the asphalt back to the main road. I watched him go for a long time. Nothing interrupted the view out here. He was probably forgetting me already, his mind back in Buenos Aires, even while I could still see his car.

There was a bench on one side of the metal building. I sat there with my suitcase and watched the sun coming up behind the row of airplanes, which had an alert, doglike quality in the stillness. At any moment Victoria and Román would come out of the building and head for the plane, along with the rest of their little party and the pilot, some friend of theirs with a license that he had earned flying a four-seater over the province of Santa Fe. They would be cheery with relief to be escaping Buenos Aires. Butch Cassidy and the Sundance Kid had once hidden out in Patagonia for a while. They robbed a bank in Río Gallegos and then crossed the empty steppes and found a cabin in the foothills of the Andes. I had seen a comic book about it at a newsstand in Palermo Chico. There was optimism in the thought.

As a child I had taken a train with my parents out to Omaha for the funeral of my great-uncle, and the waving grass and tireless sky of the Argentine campo reminded me of Nebraska. There was little to interrupt my thoughts. I was expanding and contracting with anxiety, and there was nothing to anchor me. The sun was free of the horizon now and the silence was complete, apart from the rustling and clinking I could hear through a steam vent in the wall behind me and the flitting and chirping of small birds.

A door on metal hinges screeched open behind me and there was Román in a shabby camel coat, cupping his hands to light a cigarette. It took him a moment to see me there, sitting with my knees together beside my brown suitcase, hunched against the morning chill. His eyebrows went up slowly, and he took the cigarette from between his lips.

'Anne,' he said.

I cleared my throat. 'Román.'

'What are you doing here?'

I sat up, relaxed my shoulders, pushed my hair out of my face. 'Victoria didn't tell you?'

He had gone white. I needed Victoria to come out of the building as well. I needed the whole party to be here, and no one else, so this could be accomplished quickly, smoothly. I could hear pounding and rushing in my ears, like waves on a pebble beach.

'I really don't know about this,' he said.

I put my hand in my bag and let it rest on the handle of the unloaded gun. I smiled carefully at him. 'I won't be any trouble at all,' I said. 'I just need a lift. You know?'

'This won't work,' he said.

The door opened again, and out came Victoria and a girl with a dark pixie cut. Victoria's face was uncharacteristically grim. There was a tightness to her jaw, and then she looked over and saw me and her mouth dropped open, as if she had seen a ghost.

'No, no, no,' she said. 'I told you.'

The girl with the pixie cut looked back and forth between the two of us. A young man came through the door, turning up his collar against the breeze.

'Is this everyone?' I said.

Victoria and Román were staring at each other silently.

Victoria was shaking her head. The second young man looked puzzled.

'Is this everyone?' I said again, more loudly, my hands closing around the handle of the gun.

'Yes, just us four. Not you,' Victoria said.

'You can't be here,' Román said. 'You don't understand. This is a very stupid thing you've done.'

'I'm coming,' I said. 'I'm sorry. There's no other way.' My throat was so dry that it was difficult to form the words. At any moment someone else might come through the door, another pilot or passenger or anyone at all, and then there would be too many to manage and there would be witnesses. I drew the pistol from my bag and aimed at Victoria. A chorus of obscenities rose from the other three like sparrows from tall grass.

'Anne,' Victoria said, and I was not prepared for this, the sight of real fear in her eyes. I had never threatened anyone before. But my hand was steady.

'You're taking me with you,' I said. 'Quickly. Now. Which plane?'

Victoria and Román looked at each other again, and this time there was despair on both faces.

'What have you done?' Román said to her.

'She has to come,' Victoria said. 'I don't see any other way. We can't draw attention.'

'Look at me, not at him,' I said. 'Which plane?' I waved Victoria toward the row of planes with the barrel of the gun, the way people did in films. She shook her head briefly at Román and walked toward the second plane in the lot. The other three followed her.

'Don't run and don't yell,' I said to their backs. Behind us the building was quiet. The second man climbed into a small plane with a blue stripe and started the engines. The roar filled the air, and through the cool air churned up by the propellers Victoria looked at me with derision and pity.

'You should really have listened to me,' she said.

Our hair was battered back from our faces. My skirt flapped violently around my legs. Victoria stood with her back to this whirlwind, her arms crossed tightly across her body, and there was something I couldn't plumb in her expression.

'Get in,' I said, and then shouted it again over the noise of the propeller. She climbed into the plane and I went just behind her, shoving my suitcase ahead of me and then clambering in. I had to bend and shuffle to squeeze past the first and second rows of seats, and there was no way to do it but to bluster through those moments of vulnerability, elbows in, as if I had planned it this way. The handle of the gun felt hot in my hand. I sat in the third row with my suitcase by my feet and rested the gun across my knees. The pilot began a long and careful review of the control panel. Victoria leaned over the back of her seat and looked into my eyes.

'Put this on,' she said finally. She held out a pair of head-phones.

'What for?' I said.

'So you don't go deaf,' she said.

I put out my hand for them, and then pulled it back and shook my head. I needed to hear as much as I could. Victoria shrugged and put the headphones on herself. The engine was loud but not deafening, and I could hear stray words passing between the pilot and Román in the seat next to him. Time and weather, fuel, the sun; storms somewhere to the south. Once or twice the pilot glanced back at me. I wondered if I looked frightening. Once we had taken off I would be able to relax.

Our disparate aims would resolve into one. I wouldn't matter anymore, and the bullets that my gun did not contain wouldn't matter either. The way I had forced myself onto the plane would look, in retrospect, like an embarrassing but forgivable lapse in manners, as if I had gotten too drunk at a dinner party. Maybe there was even something droll in Victoria's expression, as if she were pleased at my spirit.

The plane rolled along the packed dirt. The pilot and Román had put on their own headphones; the girl with the pixie cut kept twisting around in her seat to stare at me and chew her nails. I could see out through the windshield to the perfectly straight lines of the runway, which ended in the sea of grass.

I had never been in a plane as small as this eight-seater Britten-Norman. It rattled and bounced lightly on the runway, like a pinewood derby car. It smelled like fuel and hot grease and the old fabric that covered the seats. The window beside me was broad and square like the window of a bus, and I looked out at the grasses sliding by. The engines kicked into a higher gear, and I began to feel the suspension and pressure that had always thrilled me on airplanes. There was a sand-colored dog running through the long grass at the edge of the strip. I watched it run joyfully, falling farther and farther behind, blurred and indistinct and the color of the earth, and then the plane lifted off from the runway and I watched the dog raise its head to follow us.

The fact of being airborne was always astonishing. The chatter between the pilot and Román had stopped. There was only the engine and the gleam of the sky through the windshield, and for a few moments we banked left and the ground disappeared. I had not expected the steep angles of flight in such a small craft. My stomach was unsettled. I was happy to be free of the city that had been closing in on me for months but I felt that I would miss it too. I hoped we would fly over it, or near it. I wanted to see it spreading out across the sodden low earth, and then the immense breadth of the Río de la Plata overtaking and dwarfing it, as I had seen it from the plane when I landed nearly nine months before.

Victoria turned again and watched me over the back of the seat. With the headphones on she looked vaguely like a wartime telephone operator. She was chewing gum, probably to keep her ears from popping, but it made her look bored, and I wondered again if I was misunderstanding which one of us was the dangerous one at this moment.

'How long will it be?' I said.

'Four or five hours,' she said. 'It depends on the wind. We'll have to refuel.'

Below us a town knitted itself together out of prairie roads and railroad tracks. The ground was a dull winter color. A meandering river shone up at us, flat and immaculate.

'Are you really a student?' Victoria said.

I felt impatient. 'Hush,' I said, and then, in English to myself, 'Christ.' She rested her head on her hands on the back of the seat, looking at me with her wide doll's eyes. She had gotten her roots touched up.

'Are you really from Toronto?' she said. 'Where did you get that gun?'

I laughed. She stared steadily at me, but I kept laughing.

'Why not be honest now?' she said.

'Why not, indeed?' I said. If she had been anyone else, she might have blushed. I couldn't guess what she was hiding now, but there was something, and she knew that I knew it.

'You wouldn't really shoot me,' she said.

206

'You're free to take your odds,' I said.

The girl with the pixie cut tugged on Victoria's jacket, giving me a frightened look, as if trying to guide a child away from a tiger enclosure at the zoo. I wondered if they were lovers. What had Román said – What have you done? That was the complaint of a cuckold if I ever heard one. There had been fatigue in his voice as well as panic. It must be hard for him, I thought now for the first time, trailing around after Victoria in a frothy wake of bewitched girls, listening while she went glassy-eyed talking about Argentine territorial integrity or whatever it was that was keeping her awake these last months. I had always been puzzled by her politics, the way she was enthralled by the symbolic but seemed so bored by the day-to-day. She disliked Onganía but seemed to see the coup as occurring on a plane of events that was fundamentally not relevant to her. She was bare-breasted Liberty astride a barricade in one of those old French paintings. Liberty carried a sword and was illuminated with heavenly light; she didn't care about beef tariffs or excise taxes.

I could see a storm now in the distance to the west, soft and gray, quite low over the land. When would I have a chance to eat again? When we stopped to refuel, I guessed. I twisted a button on my coat back and forth, trying to think what dangers the pit stop might raise and how I could manage them. Victoria might try to lose me, given the chance. Strand me on an airstrip somewhere in the upper margin of Patagonia. I would have to insist on staying in the plane while they refueled. But what if they went away and brought back the police, and I was sitting there placidly in the third row of seats with the gun across my knees? But they wouldn't. They were as afraid of the police as I was. If I could stay in the plane, I would be all right.

Back in the States I had heard of girls hitching rides on twin props, charming one pilot after another. The pilots were like truckers: they liked company, and conversation helped them stay awake. I had known a girl from Seattle who spent the summer seasons in Alaska that way, working her way from timber camps to canneries along the Pacific coast and into the tundra. Some of the California girls who came from the ranches did it too. It was exotic to me. The landscape we passed over now was the ordinary gray of a temperate winter in a rainy climate, but in a few hours we would reach the edge of one of the great cold deserts of the world.

'Will we fly over Buenos Aires?' I said to Victoria.

'Of course not,' she said. 'We haven't filed our charter. We would crash into someone.'

I said nothing.

'You'll miss it?' she said.

I glanced at her.

'You're funny,' she said, shaking her head. 'Even after all this?'

I thought of Nico. The intricacy of his knowledge, his connections, his commitment. Our peculiar alignment. I felt a rush of humiliation again at his betrayal. It must have been so easy for him to do it. I was never a real part of his world. No foreigner ever could have been. I couldn't imagine what it would be like to be rooted anywhere as deeply as Nico Fermetti was rooted in Barracas, Buenos Aires, Argentina.

'Do you have a boyfriend back home?' Victoria said.

'No.'

'You are a lonely girl,' Victoria said.

This seemed like an insolent way to talk to a woman holding a gun. She read this thought, also, in my expression. 'A lot of people are lonely,' she said quickly.

'Are you?' I said.

'Never,' she said. 'I have a purpose.'

She looked very placid when she said it. This was the kind of thing that made her seem much younger than twenty-seven.

'That doesn't make sense,' I said. 'A purpose doesn't keep you company.'

'Mine does,' she said.

I disliked her certainty. 'Do you love Román?' I said. I had to say it loudly to be heard over the droning of the plane. But the other passengers were wearing headphones, and it felt like a long way from the back of the plane to the front where the two men sat.

'Of course,' she said.

'But you lie to him. You do things behind his back.'

'Not the important things,' she said. 'With the important things we are 100 percent together.'

'What are the important things?'

She was silent again. She smiled slowly. She was pleased and jittery, as if containing some great news. I couldn't understand it. I was aware again of the gun resting on my skirt. When I reached up to smooth my hair, my skin smelled like hot metal, like a handful of change.

'Why did you come here?' Victoria said.

'To this plane?'

She rolled her eyes. 'To this country.'

'To study,' I said.

She leaned closer to me over the back of her seat. 'I should have known you were lying,' she said.

I looked out the window. The sky was a weak, shining color. I could see feathery shapes on the ground that were the long shadows of leafless windbreaks.

'When I called your apartment the first time, you sounded guilty,' she said. 'I told myself it was nothing.'

'Guilty of what?' I said.

She shrugged and subsided into her seat. That was the last we spoke for hours. The drone of the plane was hypnotic and I struggled to stay awake. The earth beneath the plane was nearly featureless, and the chill inside the Britten-Norman got into my blood and slowed me down, making me feel heavy and faintly despairing. After two hours I would have given a hundred pesos for a hot cup of coffee and a ham sandwich. I spent a third hour regretting, in great detail, my moody refusal of breakfast from the taxi driver. The fact that I was hungry made me feel incompetent. In fact, there was a heavy cloak of incompetence over everything that had happened over the last few weeks. Agents in retreat were supposed to have a certain kind of savoir faire. I had often felt competent and necessary in the Confitería del Molino, but this kind of thing, the gun and the airplane, was not my scene. Victoria's head was bent, and when I leaned forward I saw that she was reading a book of patriotic poems. This struck me as insane, perhaps the first truly insane thing I had seen her do.

The plane was so small that its transitions were abrupt; several hours into the flight we dropped steeply through a cloud bank and approached a streak on the horizon that resolved into a runway. I shook Victoria's shoulder.

'Where are we?' I said.

'Refueling,' she said.

'But where are we?'

'Comodoro Rivadavia.'

One of the oil cities of Patagonia. The airport we were approaching was stranded alone on a plain at the foot of a ridge, and a low city spread out to the south. Beyond was the ocean. It was late morning by now, but there was a dark cast to the air. The humid spring that had already begun in Buenos Aires was not evident here. The mountains below were olive drab. The plane bounced in the air, which made me feel sick.

The descent was turbulent, and I discovered that I could remember most of the words to the Lord's Prayer. Victoria was cursing softly to herself as the runway tilted and swung into view. The landing knocked me forward into the back of her seat. Nausea threatened. I collected myself while the plane taxied, checking my mouth for blood with one hand and finding my grip on the gun with the other. The young pilot was on the radio. I climbed awkwardly out of my seat and tried to reach him. I was tangled in a belt of some kind.

'Tell him not to say a word!' I yelled to Román, who was in the co-pilot's seat. 'Not a word!'

Román looked alarmed. 'He won't,' he said. 'He won't say anything.'

'The police would take you away as well as me,' I said.

'He won't say anything,' Román said again.

'Calm down, mi amor,' Victoria said to me. 'No one wants police. Please don't be agitated.'

'I'm staying in while you refuel,' I said.

'We all are, except the boys,' Victoria said.

I smoothed my hair. 'Bring food,' I called to the pilot and Román, who were climbing down from the plane. 'Do you hear me?'

The refueling took a long time. I had to pee. There was no good way to take care of it. The men were gone for thirty minutes, maybe forty-five. Could I climb down and crouch on the tarmac under the plane? Out across the long runway, crews of luggage men went to and fro with carts. A group of mechanics in green coveralls worked on a Boeing a hundred yards away. I would look crazy, squatting under the plane. It would draw attention. The airport terminal loomed.

'Victoria, do you have to use the bathroom?' I said.

She looked back at me with intense relief. 'In the most terrible way,' she said.

'Okay, we both go,' I said. 'You stay with me. All right?'

'Anything, anything.'

The girl with the pixie cut wanted to come too. We climbed down and began the long walk to the terminal. I put the gun in my purse but kept my fingers on it. The mechanics in the green coveralls waved at us, blew kisses. The sun had nearly come out; it was a hot white spot in the low sky. The two girls walked ahead of me.

The inside of the terminal was bustling, tidy. A row of navy officers in uniform sat along the bar of the café, reading newspapers. We found an empty ladies' room at the far end and, after some hesitation, I hung my purse with the gun in it from the hook on the back of the stall door. Everything I did while in possession of the gun was made ridiculous by it.

I washed my hands at the basin alongside Victoria and the other girl, the weighted purse sliding insistently down over my hip. Victoria studied herself in the polished steel mirror and adjusted the pin in her hair.

'I saw a stand with croissants,' the girl said.

'Can we?' Victoria said.

We bought bags of chocolate croissants and beef empanadas. I paid. 'My treat,' I said. I felt delirious. The girls were both glassy-eyed. We pushed through the revolving doors and walked back to the plane, tearing into the bags as we went. The sun had come out and we seemed to be walking into an utterly empty planet that had nothing but the bare mountains and the little Britten-Norman in it.

The boys were waiting for us in the plane. They had bought pastries as well, and we sat in silence for a few minutes, eating. I felt warm again, and hopeful. There were crumbs in my hair.

I decided that when we were in the air again I would tell them there were no bullets in the gun.

We taxied, waited twenty minutes for the all-clear from the tower, and took off. The mountains below us looked velvety in the sunlight, wrinkled and soft like the hide of an animal. The plane banked and I was blinded by the sun streaming in the window. I thought again that I might vomit, and groped around under my seat for the paper bag that the croissants had come in. I bent down to look for it and felt cold air streaming in through a bolt-hole at my heel. I tried not to think too hard about it. The plane turned east. The bay of Comodoro Rivadavia, ringed with white, disappeared behind us. I looked down into the deep blue of open ocean. I felt a rush of fear.

Victoria was looking at me over the back of her seat again. 'Why don't you give me that pistol,' she said.

'Why are we over the ocean?'

She held out her hand. Her nails were painted pink.

'Where are we going?' I said.

'There are four of us,' she said. 'There is one of you. Just give it to me.'

'That's not how it works,' I said. Over her shoulder I could see the girl with the pixie cut, whose name seemed to be Silvia, watching the two of us. 'Just tell me where we're going.'

'You can't fly this plane,' Victoria said. 'So you can't kill anyone.'

213

'That's ridiculous. I can kill everyone but the pilot.'

I tried to see what Román and the pilot were doing. The backs of their heads gave nothing away.

'You know you won't shoot anyone,' she said.

'Tell me where we're going,' I said.

'It may upset you.'

'Why aren't we going to Ushuaia? Where are we going?'

'No one's destiny is in Ushuaia,' she said.

'Mine is,' I said. 'My destiny is absolutely in Ushuaia, you lunatic.'

There was a lurch and a crash of pain. When I opened my eyes again I was on the floor, or not quite on the floor but wedged between the seats, with blood in my hair and on the left side of my face, and my head was throbbing. I turned with great difficulty and looked up. Victoria was framed against the white light at the window. In one hand she held a wrench with my blood on it, and in the other she held my gun.

'This is too light,' she said, waving the .22.

'Ow,' I said.

She opened the chamber and gave me a look of deep disappointment.

'Aahh,' I said. I had forgotten Spanish and most of English. 'You hit me.'

'There are no bullets in the gun,' she called over her shoulder to the others. She dropped it on the seat and leaned over me. She was kneeling, like a child on a school bus craning to see a fight. 'We are going to the Malvinas. You should not have come.'

'What – what for?' I said.

'To tear down the English flag,' she said, and then she smiled, and she was radiant.

For an hour I lay in the back seat, lifting my hand every so often to feel the blood coagulated in my hair, assuring myself it had not begun to bleed again, and trying to think what to do. I lay dreaming like that, defeated.

'How will you get away?' I said finally.

Victoria glanced over at me. 'They will take us away.'

'Who?'

'The English navy, you idiot.'

'That's what you want?'

'We want to tear down the flag. Sacrifice ourselves for la patria.'

'Sacrifice?'

'Revolutionaries often go to prison.'

I thought again about vomiting.

'I think you're a spy,' Victoria said.

I wondered if I was about to die. Would they do it here, on the plane? It would be messy in a small space.

'I told you not to come,' Victoria said. 'You didn't listen to me.'

'I'm not a spy,' I said weakly. 'What flag, anyway?'

'We'll find one. We're landing in Stanley. It's the capital. There must be flags.'

For another hour I said nothing. I was trying not to fall asleep. I probably had a concussion. I could see that the English would arrest us instantly when we arrived. Everything depended on whether I could get separated from the others and convince someone to let me get Gerry on the phone.

'I don't understand why you're doing this,' I muttered to Victoria. 'I don't see what it's good for.' Why does the KGB care about restoring the Falklands to Argentina, was what I meant to say. What does it matter to them?

'I said you shouldn't have come,' she said.

'I just don't understand it,' I said. 'Why would they help you do this?'

She looked back at me over the seat. 'They?'

I said nothing further. Everything was off, tilted to the side.

'You've behaved very badly,' she said. 'Back at the airport, I thought you might ruin everything. But now I see it doesn't make any difference that you're here.'

She picked up the book of poems again. The sun was going down by then, and the light in the plane was honey-colored. She looked like a government poster for literacy.

She was not KGB. None of them were.

I propped myself up, drawing in a deep breath. Victoria didn't look up, and I lay down again. The pain in my head made it hard to think.

None of them were KGB. They were just students, acting out a fantasy about la patria. The only agent on that plane was me, and I was fighting a proxy war against no one.

'There it is,' Silvia said. 'I see it.'

I pushed myself up and looked out the window. Below us, in the slanting light, a new horizon rose from the sea. The tension in the airplane lifted. They were joyful. Afraid, but also joyful. The plane bumped through the air as if over a country road. We were beginning to drop.

Victoria hummed to herself. I touched the crusted blood over my ear again.

The Falkland Islands, the Malvinas, opened up beneath us. Dusk was gathering over the ocean and a few lights twinkled already along the coast. A port and a handful of white houses appeared, and then steadily drifted away beneath us. Two white roads threaded through a dun expanse like an English moor.

For a few minutes we seemed to be following one of the roads, meandering slightly to match the way it curved through a low mountain range. The land was empty. I remembered that there were only a few thousand people living here.

'What is all this for, Victoria?' I said. 'Don't you see there's nobody here?'

'It's for Argentina.'

'What does Argentina need this rock for?'

'It's not for the rock,' she said. 'It's for the idea.'

We were passing over the interior. Far to the south I could see the Atlantic gilded by the sunset, but the land below us seemed to swallow light. I thought I could see a single white truck on the road beneath us. It rolled and rolled through low, treeless mountains. There were no buildings anywhere.

At last Stanley appeared. There was a narrow bay like a fjord, gleaming in the late sun, and beside it, when my eyes adjusted, there was a patch of gridded streets where tiny yellow lights were beginning to come on. The plane droned on. The town looked lonely and small with the dimming interior at its back. I wondered if Victoria and company might be foiled in their mission by a sheer lack of witnesses. What if they got out of the plane and found a flag to tear down and no one noticed? I stared intently at the town. We were beginning to bank. I couldn't see much on the water. No ships at anchor in the bay. A few jetties reached into the water, flanked by boats. I searched the ground for signs of the airport. The Britten-Norman was circling, corkscrewing lower, but I couldn't tell where we were headed.

'Where's the airport?' I shouted to Victoria. The engines were growing louder as we descended.

'There is none,' she said.

'What?'

'There is none,' she said, as if this information were not at all interesting. 'There's no airport on the whole island. Everything comes by sea.'

All the blood rushed to my face. 'Where the hell are you going to land?' I said.

'We're looking for a place,' she said. 'Someplace flat,' she added.

I hadn't considered that I might die in this particular way. I gripped the vinyl seat and thought of my mother.

'Are you trying to kill yourselves?' I said.

'Of course not,' Victoria said.

Silvia was fishing under her seat. She straightened up and brushed her hair out of her face; she was holding a square blue-and-white package, the Argentine flag folded so that the golden sun showed. The boys in the front were chattering excitedly to each other, but I couldn't make out what they were saying. We were circling lower and lower. I could see cars now, and the shrubbery in front yards. The spire of a church passed beneath us. An ambulance – a red cross painted on the roof – crept along a narrow street.

'But if we can't–' I offered, but couldn't finish the sentence.

We headed out over the bay, then inland again. The pilot shouted something, and Victoria said, 'There's a soccer field.' She leaned forward. 'On a soccer field there won't be any flag to tear down,' she said. 'But we can lay this one out, anyway.'

I couldn't see a soccer field. Through the right-side window I could see only blocks of houses. The plane shuddered. I covered my face with my hands.

'Nacho is a great pilot,' Victoria said. 'Once he landed on a lake in Bariloche.'

218

The soccer field slid into view from the south, a brown rectangle bordered on one side by the last houses of Stanley, on the other side by a hurricane fence that faced into the rolling plain. The pilot would have to set the plane down between the houses and the fence; it was a distance of perhaps a hundred yards. My mind was blank with fear. Victoria was holding my hand. The view through the windshield of the Britten-Norman was only earth now. A blue car turned onto the narrow street that girded the field, and then stopped, and a person got out and looked up. We were so low that I could see he was wearing a scarf. The nose of the plane jerked upward. My head started to bleed again. A torrid sunset filled the windshield, and then two white houses, side by side, in ordinary human scale, and then we hit the ground and rolled.

I was thrown to the floor by the landing and struggled to get into my seat again while Nacho wrestled with the plane. It took only a few seconds to come to a stop. I crawled up onto the seat, but I was dizzy, and I sank forward and pressed my face into the back of Victoria's seat. My feet were braced on the floor. I began to be aware of my body again, feet and hands, seething gut. The engines cut out. Silence descended over all of us.

Victoria was saying something but I couldn't make it out. I could hear her voice in the ringing quiet, but her words wouldn't resolve. I watched her turn toward me and back toward Román, who was clambering back over the seats. She looked frightened and thrilled. They were all talking at once now and none of it made any sense, like the chatter of birds. Victoria pulled a handkerchief from her coat, balled it into my hand, and pressed it to my head. I looked down at my dress. My left shoulder was stained black with blood.

We climbed down out of the plane onto the soccer pitch. My

knees were shaking. Our faces were filled with orange light. Silvia and Victoria and Román spread the flag out on the cold ground, singing and crying. Their shadows were twenty feet long, reaching toward the darkness that came over the hills behind us. A small crowd was forming in the street that edged the field to the north. I could see them gathering, conferring. There was a woman in a kerchief, two men in overcoats. I thought I was cold, but I still couldn't feel my body very well.

The four young Argentines linked arms. They must have looked striking from the street, standing behind the flag, ten feet of pale blue nylon spread out on the ground, the white plane at rest behind them on the pitch. I stood off to the side, thinking, breathing quickly. It had been five minutes now since we had landed. The cluster of men and women was beginning to come across the street. Neighbors were coming out of houses up and down the block. Victoria and Román and Silvia and Nacho swayed back and forth, singing the himno nacional. I folded the handkerchief that was in my hand and tied it over my head so it covered the wound on my temple.

'Who are you? What is this?' a man called out. English voices. There was a sharp evening wind in our faces that smelled like the ocean. In the distance, a siren was going off.

'Vinimos por la patria,' Victoria called out.

'Who are you?' called a woman. 'Is this some kind of a joke?'

'A derrotar el imperialismo inglés,' Román shouted.

There were two dozen people on the pitch now, and more coming. I clutched my coat around myself. A tremor was running down my back and legs.

'The police are coming,' a man said.

'This stupid bloody business,' said a woman near me. Victoria and Román and their friends sang and shouted in Spanish, pink-cheeked, euphoric. The woman closest to me was staring at me curiously, as if I were a member of a species not only alien to her but also clearly alien to the four young Argentines on the pitch. She wore glasses with thick frames and a man's wool hat, pulled on hastily over curled hair.

'Hello,' I said. She started.

'You speak English,' she said. Then, 'What's happening here?'

It seemed pointless to try to answer that. Behind her, a dark sedan with a flashing light on the roof turned off the road and drove slowly onto the grass, followed at a block's distance by a second. Victoria raised her arms and crossed her wrists, as if to welcome her arrest. A man came up behind the woman in glasses and peered at me.

'You could have killed someone,' he said, 'flying that damn thing in here.'

My head was bleeding again. I pressed my hand to it. Policemen climbed out of the two cars, which were parked at angles to each other, their lights flashing silently. A third car appeared at the end of the street. I was dizzy.

'She's bleeding,' somebody murmured.

The policemen were handcuffing Nacho and Román. Victoria was the last to go, and just before they put the cuffs on her she dived at the ground and snatched up the flag. The wind caught it, and it billowed like a sail. Then someone pulled it out of her grip and twisted her arms behind her back.

The woman in glasses put her hand on my sleeve and stared into my face. 'Harry,' she said, and the man with her stepped forward and grasped my other arm. The three of us gazed solemnly at each other.

'It's all right,' I said, and then, without knowing that I was going to say it, 'I just want to lie down.'

'She's American,' the woman said. 'Harry, I don't understand it.'

The tallest and heaviest of the policemen cuffed me. 'Where's this blood coming from?' he said, turning my hand palm-up, which twisted it uncomfortably against the small of my back.

'She's bleeding from the head,' the woman said.

The policeman walked me toward the last car. Strands of my hair blew across my face, into my mouth. The other four had been driven away already. Dark was falling quickly.

'Is this a joke?' a male voice said, but I couldn't tell if he was speaking to me.

In the car I stared silently at my knees. The ringing in my ears hadn't stopped, and I felt sweaty and faint. The officer in front kept looking at me in the rear-view mirror. I could feel blood pooling in my ear.

'Where do you come from?' said the officer on the passenger side.

I said nothing. I remembered the story of the U-2 pilot who was shot down over the Soviet Union. He ejected from the plane and a group of villagers found him sitting in a turnip field, having fallen thirteen miles with a silk parachute.

'She's in shock,' said the driver.

'Is the doctor in?' said the other.

'He'll have heard by now.'

We got out of the car in front of a small gray building, identified over the door with the word HOSPITAL. The emergency ward was a little room divided in two with a curtain; I was the sole patient. A ruddy doctor examined me, speaking in an odd Falklander burr to the two policemen, who waited respectfully on the other side of the curtain. A nurse appeared with a thermos full of tea and a blanket. The doctor shined a light in my eyes.

'She's concussed,' he said. 'She'll need a rest and fluids. A few stitches as well.' He clicked the light off and considered me. 'Well, that'll be a story,' he said.

He shaved a patch above my ear so he could stitch up the cut. Afterward, while I lay back in the bed with my scalp numb and my brain beginning to throb again, the nurse would not let me go to sleep. 'Dangerous,' she said. She was small, gray-haired, her smock hastily buttoned over a housedress. 'I was roasting a chicken. Wasn't expecting this tonight.' She sat beside me for an hour, reading a magazine, while an IV bag dripped into my veins. I started to return to myself, although the lights in the room were bleary, and voices in the hallway had a warped quality.

The policemen came back, and the nurse excused herself.

'Perhaps you could explain what happened here this evening,' said the taller one. He was standing against the light, which was much too bright; I squinted painfully at him.

'Call the CIA,' I croaked.

'The what?'

I pushed myself up on my elbows and felt the tug of the IV. 'Is this an English jurisdiction?' I said.

'Yes.'

'Call Gerald Carey,' I said. 'I'm CIA.'

They looked at each other. The shorter of the two men walked slowly to the door that led to the hallway and pulled it shut.

'The other four say they're here to take back the islands for Argentina,' observed the taller man.

'When I got on the plane with them,' I said with great deliberation, 'I was mistaken about the purpose of the trip.'

I tried to start at the beginning, but the story was filled

223

with switchbacks and the two men kept interrupting me with questions. The shorter man was taking notes in a book, and he kept scratching out what he had written and turning to a fresh page. The nurse appeared with sandwiches for them, the smell of which turned my stomach, although I was hungry. She had not yet given me anything to eat.

'Why does the CIA give a damn about these kids?' said the shorter man finally.

'We thought they were KGB,' I said.

'KGB? This nonsense with the flag?'

'Well, it looks like we were wrong,' I said, closing my eyes. It wasn't until years later, when all the statutes of limitations had expired and the Falklands Invaders were being frank in interviews, that I learned what the target of the July bombing plot had been. It was a statue of Sir Francis Drake that was under construction at that time in one of the parks along the waterfront. Román had felt that to honor an English pirate while Argentine islands were under the yoke of the English Navy was too much to bear. They had planned to set off the bomb on Argentina's Independence Day, the ninth of July.

By the next morning, when I woke in the Stanley hospital with the worst headache of my life, the incident was in the international pages all over the world under the heading FALKLANDS INVASION. There was a picture of Victoria mugging happily at the camera from the single jail cell in Stanley she shared with her co-conspirators, the flag wrapped around her shoulders. I didn't see it until later. A cable came from the State Department overnight, requesting safe passage home for me, and that my name and photo be withheld.

OCTOBER 1966. STANLEY, FALKLAND ISLANDS

The Falklands police arranged for me to get to Chile on an English fishing tub. Two days later I watched the sun rise over a gray ocean from the deck of the Fitzroy. I had never been so sick in my life. The sailors were amused, then concerned, as I turned green and weak. I mooned for death on a cot in the stern. It took days for me to get my legs, to keep down a few pieces of bread and a can of sliced peaches. On the fourth day I woke with a steady gut and stepped out onto the icy deck to see the ocean slashed and pitted with the islands of Tierra del Fuego. We were in the Strait of Magellan. Colonies of penguins massed chattering at the water's edge. The oldest sailor and the sole Spanish speaker on board, who was from the Chilean side of Patagonia, explained his mother's method for pickling penguin meat while he hauled up nets full of sub-Antarctic fish. I couldn't tell if he was having me on or not. The cook offered hot coffee, and for the first time I gladly accepted it and didn't vomit over the railing afterward. The ocean was pink to the east, a faint oily pink over a deep gray, and I could see what made people accept this life. It was the feeling of being nowhere. Being nowhere for a long time and continuing to sleep and eat and watch sunrises anyway.

In the strait, the boat lingered on pewter water between bare headlands that were traced with snow. For a whole afternoon we passed slowly by a glacier, a mass of unearthly blue ice that girdled a black mountain and ran down its lap into the sea. The sailors were casual in this landscape, working and chatting, but every time I came up on the deck the cold excoriated me and the mountains made me feel that we were in the presence of ancient forces that were disturbed by our passage. I hid out below-decks, playing endless games of rummy, taking comfort in the cans of beets and the reeking socks strung on a clothesline made of twine, the pages from dirty magazines neatly cut out and tacked up over the stove. Someone had given me an old coat and a hat with earflaps. I felt tired to my bones. How long had I been so tired?

I said before that the night I ran out on my mother, I made one stop before I drove to Baltimore. I thought of it again while the boat drifted over its fishing nets at the end of the world.

That night, I left the Packard under a horse chestnut tree at the end of Joanne's block and approached her house on foot. It was only about seven o'clock in the evening, but it had been dark for hours. I was still wild from the fight, my heart racing, sweating under a light wool coat. My lip throbbed where my mother had hit me, and my knuckles throbbed from hitting back. I circled around to the backyard of their big old house and picked up a handful of acorns from under a tree. Joanne's light was on. I threw the acorns at the glass until a shadow appeared, and the sash lifted with a squeak.

'Vera?'

'It's me, come down, will you?'

The window closed and I waited in the dark. I kept opening and closing my sore fist. If I had done that, I might do anything.

226

I could do anything. Joanne appeared in silhouette at the back door, pulling on a coat, and then quietly closed it behind her and hurried across the grass.

'What happened? Are you all right?' she said.

'God, I really miss you,' I said.

'You're going to get me in trouble,' she said, but her voice was warm. She glanced back at the house.

'I'm not going home,' I said. 'My mother got my grades and she hit me and I hit her back. I can't go back there. She'll kill me. Or I'll kill her.'

I could just make out the pale oval of Joanne's face in the dark, the small mouth, and I could see that she was looking me over to see if I'd been hurt. She brushed my hair out of my face and turned me toward the faint yellow of the streetlamps. 'She split your lip.'

'Come with me,' I said. 'I'm going to Baltimore. I'll get a job.'

'You're running away?'

That sounded too juvenile. 'I'm leaving. I'll get my own place. I have some money in the bank.' I had two hundred dollars, years of Christmas money saved from my grandparents.

'What about school?'

'I'm failing school anyway.' I could see it so clearly, an apartment for the two of us, me working as a secretary somewhere, Joanne with her painting things set up in a corner where she could get the light. We had talked about this future, a fantasy of our adult lives, in some space before the real business of living began. But I needed it now. 'Come with me,' I said again, and because she didn't seem to understand what I meant, because she was hesitating as if this were not a matter of life and death, I kissed her.

It was as if I had been picked up by a wave and left in a heap on the beach. I drifted back from the kiss, overcome, with fresh tears in my eyes. She was looking at me; she was immobile, and her pale face, when it resolved in the darkness, was shocked.

'Why did you do that?' she said. She took a step backward. I couldn't think of anything to say. She touched her lip with her fingers.

'What's the matter with you?' she said. 'My mother thought – but I told her you weren't – you weren't like that.'

I was falling through the ground, into a pit. I turned and walked quickly away. I wanted to vomit. Behind me there was no sound. She didn't come after me, she didn't move. She said nothing.

By the time I saw the lights of Baltimore that night, my head throbbed from crying and my mouth was dry, and I knew I would never speak to her again. There was a pain in my chest; I kept putting my hand over it as I drove. Joanne was the last person who could look at me and see me looking back, who could put out her hand and find me there. I wouldn't let it be so easy again.

It wouldn't be clear for some time that I would never live in my mother's house again, but I think I knew that too, that night. There was simply no way to go back. The past is a foreign country, as they say. I lived for nearly a decade as if I had come from nowhere. But there are so many ways to cross a border.

It was weeks to our destination in Chile. I was wearing a spare oilcloth suit when we drifted at last around the Playa Ancha and into the port of San Antonio. I had lost ten pounds and my hands and face were red and rough from the relentless salt in the wind. The ground kept moving beneath me for days after we landed. It moved while I paid for a seat in a minibus headed east, while I haggled with a hotelier in a Santiago street so narrow that the delivery boys on motorbikes put their hands out to brush the wall as they went around the corner. It kept moving while I called Gerry's number from one pay phone after another through the Barrio Brasil. When I reached him at last, he said he was so relieved to hear from me that he didn't know what to say.

'You left me to die,' I said. I was standing at a pay phone next to a fruit cart, and the vendor was holding out a luminous melon in my direction.

'I did everything I could,' he said. 'We were all shocked at how fast things shut down. They arrested three of ours that first week. We couldn't be more aggressive.'

'You did nothing for me,' I said.

His voice changed, became smooth. 'You're angry.'

'I expect hazard pay.'

'You'll get it.'

He wired me, in four separate installments over the course of three days, my final payment for the job. It was more money than I had ever had at one time; it was more money than I had ever seriously considered. I changed hotels immediately, in case someone had noticed all the trips I was making to the Western Union office. I spent three days in the most beautiful hotel in Santiago, reading newsstand paperbacks and ordering room service on a balcony that overlooked a park. Old men sat on a bench across the street, under a spreading plane tree, gossiping and smoking cigars. In the mornings, a bellhop would knock on the door with the paper. It was on that balcony that I read an item in the Cono Sur pages of the morning news:

ARGENTINE STUDENTS RELEASED
ONGANÍA REFUSES EXTRADITION

The protagonists of the so-called Falkland Islands Invasion have been released from a Buenos Aires prison on condition of time served, having spent twenty-two days as prisoners...

And a photo: Victoria in front, beaming, hand raised in a modest wave, the coat that I remembered folded over her arm. Román a half-step behind, easy to overlook. The other co-conspirators carefully watching their feet as they came down the prison steps.

I spent my mornings at the visa office, the American consulate, Pan Am. I was using my real passport now. I was Vera Kelly again.

When I thought about the flight home, even though I knew that I would be flying in a reliable commercial jet, I was tormented by images of the shuddering Britten-Norman, the soccer field sliding into view. Whenever I saw the envelope on the vanity with the airline tickets in it, my chest tightened and my pulse raced. I told the concierge at the hotel that I was afraid to fly, and asked if he knew a doctor. He understood me perfectly. Within an hour I was standing in a dim consulting room in the back of a gaudy apartment just across the park, with a doctor who took his prescription pad out of a drawer before I even removed my coat.

'I'm nervous about flying,' I said.

'You would like half a dozen, or a dozen?' he said.

I hesitated. 'A dozen.'

It was because of these pills, the first one taken in the taxi on the way to the airport, that I didn't flinch when the man at passport control glanced up at me, paged through my documents twice, and then said, 'You have no entry stamp.'

'Hm?' I said.

'No entry stamp,' he said. 'Where did you come from?' Because of the pill, the air between myself and the young man was filled with a sweet, benign substance, which muffled his speech and my speech and the commotion of the other passengers around us. 'I came from New York,' I said, smiling gently. I took my passport out of his hand, as if he had been offering it, which he had not. 'They didn't stamp me on the way in?'

He frowned and then looked at my other papers, the receipt showing that I had paid the airport fee, the special round of taxes, the visa with its raised seal.

'It appears they did not,' he said.

I yawned. 'Should I wait here?' I said, looking around.

He looked past me at the impatient line. 'No, miss,' he said. 'Enjoy your journey.'

NOVEMBER 1966. CROWN HEIGHTS, BROOKLYN, NEW YORK

I was packing up my apartment on Eastern Parkway when the bell rang. I went to the window and looked down. A light snow crusted the branches of a bare dogwood beside the stoop below. A hat and overcoat shifted slightly on the top step. From the third floor I couldn't see his face, but by the way he stood I knew it was Gerry. I had left two letters from him unopened in the three weeks since I came home.

I had to go down to answer the door. The front hallway was as cold as the street.

'Vera,' he said.

His expression was uncertain. That was rare for him. I wondered if it was an affectation.

'Can I come up?' he said.

We climbed the stairs in silence. I regretted, when I let him into my apartment, the fact that he would see the packing boxes, the dishes and teacups wrapped in newspaper. I left him in the sitting room and put a kettle on the stove.

'I thought you might come by to see me when you got back,' he said.

'Well, I didn't,' I said.

'I guess I'm wondering why.' The floor creaked behind me.

He had come to the kitchen doorway.

I shut a cabinet. 'I've said all I meant to say. I'm finished with this.'

He sighed. He looked pained, but only a little, as if I were ending a romance that hadn't been fun in a long time.

'We've invested a lot in you,' he said.

'Not so much, in the end,' I said.

He clucked. 'Is that it? You're hurt that we didn't send in the cavalry for you? It's childish, Vera.'

'It's not that you didn't send in the cavalry. It's that you made me think that you had. I could have died down there, waiting for it.'

I disliked looking at him. There was a pack of cigarettes I kept over the stove. I retrieved it and lit one, and then bumped the kitchen window open half an inch, so that both of us felt an icy draft hiss across the room.

'I suppose it suited your purposes,' I said. 'It kept me there a while longer.'

Both his hands were in his pockets. He was angled toward me, one shoulder forward, as if facing into a wave.

'Have you ever done fieldwork, Gerry?' I said.

'Yes, I have.'

'The better a person is, the easier they are to lie to. Have you noticed that?' I pulled the sash up an inch higher.

Gerry said, 'It's a war, Vera.'

'That's the thing, Gerry. It's not. It's a game.'

For a minute or two neither of us said anything. I could hear gospel music coming through the ceiling.

'Where are you going?' Gerry said at last, looking over his shoulder at the stacked boxes around the sofa.

'None of your concern,' I said. 'And I'll be very happy there.'

233

JANUARY 1967. 122 MIDWOOD STREET, BROOKLYN, NEW YORK

It was my own, a townhouse on Midwood Street that I bought with cash. It took all the money from the job. I had to fix the roof, and the radiators leaked, but it had tall windows and a back garden with a flagstone path among rosebushes, and dark cherry floors that felt, somehow, always warm to the touch.

I sent my mother a letter with my new address. It had been such a long time; I was a new person now. It was possible that we were both new people. She wrote me back and invited me for the weekend. I considered it for days, then wrote her again and suggested Easter instead. I might face Chevy Chase better in the springtime.

I found a job at a television station, where I worked on the five o'clock news broadcast. I typed up scripts and answered the telephones at first. After a while I was writing scripts, and then editing.

Once, reviewing film from a demonstration in Mexico, I thought I saw Victoria, a blonde girl with a gleeful smile in the midst of a roiling mass of people, police swarming in from the side. I wound the film back several times, and each time it looked less like her. Later, I heard she had a bit part in a movie that made the festival rounds, but I never saw it.

I worked all the time. I grew clematis on a trellis in my backyard. I romanced a poet who taught English at Brooklyn College, and she cooked for me and left notes in my bed and kitchen cabinets and sticking out from behind the picture frames in my front hallway. There were cartoons of me: tall and severe, with an undermining riot of curly hair. And of her: she drew herself short and round, with sticks for legs, making a little joke of herself. She was beautiful, actually. I could never be sure if she knew it.

In the spring I found a nest in the old dovecote on my roof. There were two mottled brown eggs in it that I couldn't identify, much too big for pigeons. I never saw the mother, but in my attic room, while I waited for the eggs to hatch above me, I sometimes heard the brief beating of strong wings.

Acknowledgements

I owe thanks first of all to Soumeya Bendimerad Roberts, for seeing what this book needed, and to Masie Cochran, for knowing how it should be shaped. To Nanci McCloskey and Sabrina Wise, for their energy and good humor, and to Jakob Vala, for conjuring Vera's face. As always, I depend on my first readers for their insight and rigor: Bonnie Altucher, Tom Cook, Jenna Evans, and Helen Terndrup.

Permanent thanks to my family, who took me seriously when it would perhaps have been wiser not to, and to Mark, who is playing for keeps and yet never keeps score.

Book Club Questions

How would you describe Vera Kelly?

Do any of these qualities make Vera a better (or worse) spy?

What did you think of the jumps between Vera's past and present

How does Vera's adolescence inform her present predicaments?

How does Vera's estrangement from her mother influence her?

In noir novels and films, sexuality tends to follow certain tropes. Do you think that's the case in Who Is Vera Kelly? Is there a femme fatale in this book?

Vera's options for financial survival are restricted by both her gender and her sexuality. How might her story have played out differently ten years earlier? Ten years later?

What did you make of Vera's relationship with James? Were you ever suspicious of his reasons to be in Argentina?

What does Vera see in Victoria? What does Victoria see in Vera?

How does Vera's perspective on the Cold War change over the course of the book?

Lots of girls grow up reading Harriet the Spy and Nancy Drew novels. Why do you think there are so few adult spy novels starring female spies?

What do you think is next for Vera Kelly?

To be the first to hear about new books and exclusive deals
from Verve Books, sign up to our newsletters:
vervebooks.co.uk/signup

VERVE
BOOKS